"I told ... say y... enough?"

Ross shook his head. "Not always," he replied in a voice tinged with melancholy. "I'm a rolling stone, Sarah. I can't offer you anything permanent or lasting."

"Why are you telling me all this?" she asked impatiently.

"I just don't want there to be any misunderstandings."

She raised her hands to his face, her fingers tracing the bony ridge of his jawline, the deep clefts at the sides of his mouth, the high cheekbones, and she smiled at him.

"Fair enough," she said. "I'll consider myself warned. Now, are you going to kiss me again or not?"

Rosemary Hammond grew up in California, but has since lived in several other states. Rosemary and her husband have traveled extensively throughout the United States, Mexico, the Caribbean and Canada, both with and without their two sons. She enjoys gardening, music and needlework, but her greatest pleasure has always been reading. She started writing romances because she enjoyed them, but also because the mechanics of fiction fascinated her and she thought they might be something she could do.

The Perfect Male
Rosemary Hammond

Harlequin Books

TORONTO • NEW YORK • LONDON
AMSTERDAM • PARIS • SYDNEY • HAMBURG
STOCKHOLM • ATHENS • TOKYO • MILAN
MADRID • WARSAW • BUDAPEST • AUCKLAND

ISBN 0-373-17319-9

THE PERFECT MALE

First North American Publication 1997.

Copyright © 1996 by Rosemary Hammond.

CHAPTER ONE

SARAH, still in her robe and slippers, stood at the front window that faced the ocean, sipping her morning coffee and gazing out at the huge waves whipping the desolate shore, the tall firs and cypresses that surrounded the house swaying under the force of the strong south wind, which had already begun to whistle through every chink in the small frame cottage.

There was going to be a storm, a terrific one from the looks of it. She glanced up at the heavy canopy of black clouds that had been moving in fast since daybreak and even now was darkening the angry gray sea.

Sarah had lived in the beach cottage with her father since early childhood. She knew it had weathered many such storms, and far from being frightened, she had always found them invigorating, even exciting. But now that her father was gone, she'd have to face this one alone, and a sharp pang pierced her heart at the reminder of his sudden death just six months ago.

She could still hardly believe he was gone, and although she had been quite firm in her decision to continue his work, studying the marine wildlife here on the rugged Washington coast, it had turned out to be a heavier burden than she'd realized. Without his firm, quiet confidence to guide her, she'd come to have serious misgivings about her ability to do the work on her own, or, even more importantly, to withstand the loneliness and isolation.

Right now, however, there were several things she had to do to prepare for the threatening storm. This one seemed to be shaping up into a real monster, with gusts already coming at fifty or sixty miles an hour.

She drained her coffee, set the cup on the table and hurried into the bedroom to get dressed in a pair of sturdy jeans and heavy pullover. The rain had started, slashing now against the windowpanes and drumming on the roof.

She pulled on her boots, tied a scarf around her head and buttoned up in a waterproof anorak. When she opened the front door, she was almost swept off her feet by a sudden strong gust. Outside, battling her way against the wind, her head bent, she dashed around fastening shutters and moving small objects to shelter.

After bringing in several loads of firewood, she went to the closet under the stairs and pulled out the oil lamps and camp stove. The electricity could be off for days, and even now the lights were flickering ominously.

Candles, she thought, and ran to the kitchen where they were usually kept. There seemed to be a good supply, and as she was setting them on the counter, she glanced out the window to see that the gate at the end of the garden was banging loose. She hated the thought of going out in that gale again, but neither did she want to have to replace the gate when it was over. Any small object could be picked up by that wind and hurled through a window.

The rain was pelting down in earnest now. She ran down the path to the gate with the wind howling in her ears, the roar of the surf thundering in the background. She fastened the gate securely and started to fight her way back to the house, praying that the roof was as sturdy as she believed.

She'd only gone a few steps, however, when she heard a sudden loud cracking noise behind her. She whirled around just in time to watch, horrified, as a tall young cedar, which had snapped in the middle, started slowly falling toward the road in front of the cottage.

At the same instant, out of the corner of her eye, she caught a brief glimpse of a dark car speeding toward it on a collision course, heard the squeal of brakes. She stood there paralyzed, watching helplessly as the tree fell directly on top of the car, smashing into the roof with a loud, sickening whack.

Instinctively, and unmindful of her own danger, she sprinted swiftly out to the road.

The tree was far too heavy for her to think of budging. It seemed to be wedged into the roof of the car, where it had made a deep dent, and there was broken glass scattered at her feet. Stepping gingerly around it, she bent over and peered inside.

There was only one occupant, a man. He was slumped forward in the driver's seat, his head lying on the steering wheel and bleeding profusely. Quickly, she wrenched the door open. Although she knew it could be dangerous to move him she had no choice. It was either that or leave him out in the storm, possibly to bleed to death.

The problem was how to get him to the house. He seemed to be unconscious, but when she tugged at his arm, his eyes flickered open briefly, then shut again.

She put her face down close to his. "Can you move?" she shouted in his ear. When he didn't respond, she shook him by the shoulder. "Please, you must try! We've got to get out of here!"

His eyes opened again, but they seemed glazed. Shock, most likely, she thought, possibly a concussion. The blood seemed to be coming from a deep gash in his forehead. What other injuries he might have she couldn't even guess, and prayed nothing was broken.

Perhaps it would be better if she ran back to the house and telephoned for help. While she debated, however, she felt him stirring next to her, as though he had grasped the situation and was trying to get out of the car. He couldn't make it on his own, but by supporting him as best she could and pulling at him, he finally did manage to stumble out onto the road. His hand resting on the car door, he stood there for a moment as though dazed, obviously very unsteady on his feet.

She put an arm around his waist and urged him forward. "Lean on me," she called up to him. "We've got to hurry!"

Finally, with his weight resting against her, he managed a few steps, then a few more, until finally, after what seemed like hours, they reached the house, both of them soaked by now from the drenching rain. Flinging open the door, she led him inside and lowered him down on a nearby chair, then turned and fastened the door securely, shutting out the howling storm at last.

She stood for a moment gazing down at him, wondering what in the world she was going to do with him now that she had him safely inside. He was slumped forward in the chair, his head in his hands, blood seeping through his fingers. She had to get help. Surely the tiny local hospital would send an ambulance or an aid car for him, even in the storm.

She ran to the telephone, but when she lifted it, there was dead silence on the line. She jiggled the hook, but still nothing. Her mind raced wildly. She could get the car out and drive him the five miles to the village, but that would be an act of insanity in this weather. They could both end up killed. Besides, the tree that had fallen on his car was no doubt blocking the road anyway. She'd just have to do the best she could with him.

When she went back to him, he was still sitting in the same posture, but at least he didn't seem to be unconscious, and although his head was covered with blood, the worst of it seemed to have stopped. She lowered herself down on her knees before him and peered up into his face.

"Can you walk?" she asked.

He raised his head and gazed blankly at her. He blinked several times, as though trying to focus on her, then nodded and braced his hands on the arms of the chair, struggling to get up. Grasping him under his arms, she tugged at him until she'd gotten him on his feet, then led him slowly to the downstairs bedroom at the back of the house.

She stopped at the side of the bed and pulled off his heavy waterproof jacket. The plaid woolen shirt underneath it seemed to be dry enough, but his dark trousers were sopping. Was she going to have to undress him? The whole thing had been such a shock to her that it only just now occurred to her that she had wantonly risked taking a total stranger into her house. A *large* one at that.

But did she have a choice? Certainly in his present condition he was no threat to her. He could hardly stand upright on his own. Even now he was swaying unsteadily, and she reached out to grab hold of him before he fell.

It was far too late for regrets now. It was either take him in or leave him out there in his car, possibly to die, and the first thing she had to do was get that head wound cleaned up. She lowered him slowly down on the bed, then went across the hall to the bathroom to get the first-aid kit. Outside, the storm was still raging, the wind whipping through the tall branches, the rain slashing against the windows, the heavy pounding of the surf.

When she came back, she was relieved to see that somehow he had managed to remove the rest of his clothing and was lying under the covers, his wet trousers in a heap on the floor. She stood in the doorway for a moment watching him. His head was turned away from her, his eyes closed. His dark hair was matted with blood, his complexion a sickly gray. He was obviously in deep shock.

She hurried over to the bed. The first thing was to clean up the cut in his forehead, then try to make sure he had no other injuries. Then she hesitated for a moment, looking down at him. With his shoulders bare, his arms lying outside the covers beside his long form, he seemed to be quite a strong, well-built man, probably in his mid- to late thirties. And quite a good-looking one, too, with a strong, clean profile, square chin and determined jawline.

As she gazed down at him, something began to stir within her, a strange sensation she couldn't quite identify. Of course, it was unsettling to have this strange man in her house. It had been so long since she'd been around anyone besides her father and the people in the nearby village that she felt unsure of herself, disturbed by the alien presence.

But it was more than that. It seemed to be this particular man. Even in his weakened condition, half-unconscious, he gave the impression of terrific pent-up energy and strength. Then she gave herself a little shake, dismissing such wayward thoughts from her mind. Right now he needed her help. His very life depended on her.

She bent over him and reached out a hand to touch him lightly on the shoulder. When he didn't respond, she gave it a gentle shake. He groaned and turned his head toward her. His eyes flicked open, and he stared blankly up at her.

She gave him a tentative smile. "It looks as though we're stranded here for the time being," she said. "I think we'd better get that cut on your forehead cleaned up."

He blinked, his eyes glazed over, and he closed them again. "Whatever you say," he murmured hoarsely.

Panic clutched at her heart. What if he did die? She squeezed her eyes shut tight, as though that would make him go away. She couldn't cope with this, not so soon after her father's death.

But she knew she'd have to. She had no choice. With a sigh, she set the first-aid kit down on the bedside table and opened it. She took out a package of cotton pads, the bottle of disinfectant and, gritting her teeth, leaned over to brush back the sweep of heavy dark hair that had fallen over the man's forehead and began to clean the wound.

Although he still emitted an occasional low moan as she worked, he lay quite still. The cut didn't look quite so bad once she'd cleared away the caked and clotted blood. It probably wouldn't even need to be stitched up.

When she was through, she bandaged it carefully, then began to mop away the worst of the mess on his face and hair. Working slowly and as gently as possible, she became so absorbed in her task that she didn't realize his deep gray eyes had opened again and were staring fixedly up at her until she sat back to view her progress and heard him speak.

"Where am I?" he asked, frowning. "And who are you?"

His voice did sound a little stronger now, but when he tried to raise himself up, his features contorted in pain, and his head dropped back down on the pillow.

"You had an accident," she said in a low, soothing voice. "A tree came down in the storm and landed on your car. You're lucky to be alive. It just missed the driver's seat."

He raised a hand and touched the bandage on his forehead. "Well, it hurts like hell. How bad is it?"

"I'm not sure. All I can see is a rather nasty gash on your forehead. It must have happened when your head hit the steering wheel. You made it to the house pretty well on your own steam, so I don't think anything's broken." She rose to her feet. "I'll get you something for the pain. I imagine you're probably in shock, so you should stay warm and try to get some sleep. You also may have concussion, but I can't really tell."

He only nodded, closed his eyes again, and turned his head away. She gave him one last dubious look, then went back to the bathroom for the aspirin. When she returned, he seemed to be sleeping. She *hoped* he didn't have concussion, but had no way of telling for sure. She set the water and tablets down on the table, then tiptoed carefully out of the room, picking up the sodden mass of his clothing from the floor as she went.

In the small utility room off the kitchen, she hung up his wet clothes to dry, removing the contents of his pockets: a wallet, keys, a clean handkerchief, loose change and some papers. She carried them into the kitchen and set them down on the table, then got the camp stove lit and put on the kettle for tea.

While the water boiled, she sat down to go through his things. Although it made her feel rather uncomfortable to pry like that, surely she had a right to know who he was. If he should die, she thought with a shudder, she'd have to know whom to notify.

There were quite a few bills in the wallet, so the man wasn't a beggar by any means. His clothing had been of good quality, too. According to his

driver's license and credit cards, his name was
Ross Kirk, he was thirty-eight, six foot two, had
dark brown hair, gray eyes, and he lived in San
Francisco. Then what was he doing driving along
a back road in one of the remoter areas of the
Washington coast?

The shrill whistle of the boiling kettle snapped
her out of her reverie. Quickly putting his things
back together, she got up and made her tea, then
sat sipping it, pondering her situation.

It could be days before the road was cleared and
the power lines were repaired. There was plenty of
food in the cupboard, but what in the world was
she going to do with this stranger she'd brought
into the house?

By four o'clock that afternoon the wind had died
down a little, but it was already growing dark
outside and still raining. He had slept most of the
day, just lain there quietly, and each time she
checked on him, he hardly seemed to have moved
at all, was still in the same position, his dark head
turned away, his arms resting at his sides.

She stood beside the bed looking down at him,
filled with a terrible feeling of helplessness. Should
she waken him? Try to get him to eat something?
Take his temperature? What if his head wound got
infected, turned septic?

Yet he seemed quite a strong specimen, the broad
shoulders and upper arms well muscled. Once again
a strange sensation began to flutter inside her at the
sight of him lying there, so tall that his feet were
pressed against the footboard, his long legs out-

lined under the covers. He really was a most attractive man.

Just then he turned his head and his eyes flicked open. They fastened on hers for a moment with a puzzled, bleary expression, then darted around the room. He propped his elbows on the bed and began to raise himself up, but hadn't gotten far when he groaned loudly, squeezed his eyes shut and flopped his head back on the pillow, one arm lifted to cover his head.

Quickly, Sarah ran to the bed and bent over him. "What is it?" she cried.

"I'm not sure," he muttered through his teeth. "But I think I may have a cracked rib or two."

"Oh," she said with a sinking heart. Broken ribs! What should she do about that? Tape them up? How? With what?

Then he opened his eyes again and gave her a puzzled frown. "Where am I? And who are you?"

"My name is Sarah Wainwright," she said in a low, clear voice. "This is my house. You had an accident. I brought you inside because the road is blocked by the tree that fell on your car, and there's no way to get help." She spoke slowly, enunciating each word distinctly, as though to a child. "Do you understand?"

He nodded at last. "Sarah Wainwright," he murmured, then closed his eyes and seemed to be drifting off to sleep again.

"Listen," she said in a loud voice. "I think you should try to stay awake, eat something." When there was no response, she shook him gently by the shoulder. "Ross," she called, "can you hear me?"

"Yes," he replied groggily. "I hear you." He raised his head slowly and focused on her. "You're probably right." He tried to rise up again and winced. "Do you have anything to bind up these ribs? An old sheet, perhaps? Anything will do."

"Yes, of course."

She ran out to the linen closet and rummaged around until she came across a worn sheet she had saved to use for cleaning rags. Back in the bedroom, she tore it into strips, then gave him a dubious look.

"I'm afraid you're going to have to try to sit up if I'm to get these wrapped around you."

He gave her a curt nod. "Right. I'll need some help."

"Yes, of course."

She bent down and put an arm around his shoulders, bracing his head with one hand and pulling the pillows out from under it with the other, to prop them up behind him. Finally, he was in a sitting position, the covers lying in a heap around his waist, his smooth chest bare.

It was a slow, tedious job. Working as quickly as possible, she started winding the strips of sheeting around his chest where he seemed to feel the most pain, trying to tie them tightly enough to hold the ribs in position without hurting him.

"Ouch!" he yelped at one point. "The idea is to support the ribs, not crush them!"

"Well, I'm sorry," she muttered under her breath. Her own nerves were pretty frazzled by now. "I'm doing the best I can. I'm not a doctor or a nurse, you know."

"Believe me, I'd never make that mistake!"

The tension that had been building up inside Sarah during this whole awkward process now threatened to erupt into a simmering anger. Instead of being grateful that she'd probably saved his life, here he was complaining about the way she bandaged his stupid ribs! She gritted her teeth and bit her tongue to keep from telling him just that, reminding herself that the man was probably still in shock, that he'd lost a lot of blood, could be running a fever.

"There," she said, straightening up and forcing out a tight smile. "How does that feel?"

"It feels like hell!" he snapped. "How do you think it feels?"

Once again she choked back a stinging report. "Yes, I can imagine. Are you hungry? I really think you should eat something. How does your head feel?"

"Oh, stop clucking! It doesn't matter." His eyes scanned the room. "Where are my clothes?"

"Hanging up," she replied shortly. "They got soaked in the storm."

"Well, I'd appreciate it if you'd bring them back as soon as they're dry. I've got to leave."

Sarah folded her arms across her chest and gave him a withering look. "Leave! You can't leave. Although," she added dryly, "nothing would please me more, I'm afraid the road is blocked, your car is a wreck, and there's no way to call for help. Besides which, you're in no condition to get out of bed, much less walk five miles to the village."

He cocked a heavy dark eyebrow at her. "Oh? You think not?" He gave her an evil smile. "Watch me."

To her growing horror, he began to swing his legs slowly out from under the covers, gritting his teeth every inch of the way, but clearly determined to get out of bed, stark naked, right before her eyes. She stood there watching dumbly until finally he was sitting upright, his long legs dangling over the edge of the bed, his lower torso barely covered by the rumpled sheet.

Then she saw him start to sway. His eyes closed, his face paled visibly, his head slumped forward, and in a moment he would have fallen to the floor.

"Stop it!" she cried, dashing to his side. "Are you crazy?"

She pushed his head back on the pillow, then reached down and lifted his legs back on the bed. After covering him up again, she stared down at him in dismay.

His face was ashen, he was clearly unconscious, and all Sarah's anger began to leak away. He must be more seriously hurt than either of them had realized, and she hadn't a clue what to do about it. All she could do, she decided at last, was to let him sleep now and hope for the best.

It could be days before the road was cleared and the power lines were repaired. She had enough emergency supplies, the cupboard full of canned goods and plenty of candles to last for days, so her only real worry was the injured man who had stumbled into her life.

Later that evening, Sarah was just finishing up her evening meal when she heard the sudden rush of water running in the downstairs bathroom.

She dropped her fork on her plate with a clatter and jumped to her feet. The fool man had gotten out of bed! By now he could be lying on the floor unconscious, and then what would she do?

Muttering under her breath, she grabbed the lantern off the table and dashed down the hall. There he stood, just outside the bathroom door, propped up against it. He was covered in a blanket, still swaying, his teeth chattering, his tall figure ghostlike in the dim light cast by the lantern.

She set the lantern down on the hall table and ran to his side. "Are you out of your mind?" she cried, grabbing him around the waist and letting his weight fall on her. "Or do you just have a death wish?" She began to tug at him. "Come on. Lean on me. You've got to get back in that bed."

She could feel the heat from his body under the blanket as she guided him, half-stumbling, leaning heavily against her, back to bed. His skin felt as though it were on fire.

When she finally got him settled once again, she retrieved the lantern and raised it over him to take a closer look. His face was running with perspiration, her worst fears realized. He was burning up with fever.

She stood there for several minutes, gazing down at him. He lay quite still now, too still, his pale face utterly immobile. She felt so helpless. There was nothing she could do for him tonight except bathe his face, keep him warm. Tomorrow, if he wasn't any better, she'd just have to walk the five miles to the village and try to get help. A helicopter, perhaps, or a boat. Anything to get him out of here.

*   *   *

But by morning the worst seemed to have passed. The minute she got out of bed, she threw on a robe and ran down the hall to look in on her patient. She had slept downstairs on the couch in the living room so as to hear him if he cried out, and had had a restless night.

To her amazement, he was lying with his head propped up on the pillows, his head turned to the window, gazing out at the bright sunshine pouring through it. He still looked quite pale, his gaunt cheeks were covered with a dark stubble, and there were dark circles under his eyes, but when he turned toward her, she could see that the glazed look in them was gone.

"Good morning," she called chirpily, forcing out a bright smile. "You look as though you're feeling better today."

He shook his head dazedly, grimacing in pain. "If you mean I think I might live, then yes, I guess I do." His voice was weak, but he did manage to summon a ghost of a smile.

"Are you hungry?" she asked.

"As a matter of fact I am," he replied. "If you could feed me, I'd be most grateful. Then I'll be on my way."

"Well, we'll see about that after you've eaten. How do you like your eggs?"

He frowned. "No eggs. I couldn't face them just yet. Coffee and toast sound great."

"Fine. It'll only take a few minutes."

It was then she noticed the lamp burning by the side of the bed. The power must be back on. Perhaps the telephone was working, too, by now, and she'd be able to call for help.

On her way to the kitchen she stopped at the telephone in the hall and lifted the receiver. Nothing had ever sounded so wonderful as that blessed dial tone. As soon as she'd fixed his breakfast she'd call Timothy, see if he could come out to diagnose the extent of Ross's injuries.

While she was making his breakfast, she heard the water running in the bathroom, and panic clutched at her heart. Would she have to go rescue him again? The fool man! Why couldn't he just stay put? She was about to run to see if he needed help, but stopped herself. He'd seemed quite normal. If he were in trouble, surely he'd call out or she'd hear him fall.

When she came back to the bedroom with his breakfast tray, he was settled back in bed again, sitting up and unwinding the strips of sheeting she'd wrapped around his chest the night before. Although he still needed a shave badly, it looked as though he'd managed to shower and wash his hair. His color had improved, too.

"I'm afraid I got these wet in the shower," he said, glancing up at her as she set the tray down on the bedside table. "Hope you won't mind giving me a hand binding the ribs up again."

"No, of course not," she said hastily, not at all sure she wanted to come into such close contact with all that bare masculine flesh now that the emergency seemed to be over. "But the telephone is working now. I can call Timothy and hopefully he can come out here and do it properly."

"Timothy?" he asked, puzzled.

"Yes. Timothy Conroy. Our local doctor. He's a good friend of mine."

Immediately, his face shut down. "No," he said, his voice taking on a hard edge. "No doctor."

"But you need professional help," she protested. "I have no idea what to do, or how badly you're hurt."

"I don't need a doctor. I just need to get out of here."

"Well, you're certainly not well enough to leave under your own steam, not to mention that the road is probably still blocked and your car definitely out of commission. After Timothy takes a look at you—"

"No!" he broke in roughly. "No doctor. And quit fussing over me."

Stung, she drew herself up to her full five foot seven and glared down at him. "I am not fussing," she rejoined tartly. "I'm only being sensible. Actually, there's nothing I'd like better than to get you out of here, but out of simple humanity, I took you in, did my best to—"

"Humanity be damned!" he growled, and sat up a little straighter, glaring right back at her.

Their eyes locked together. Try as she might, Sarah found herself unable to look away. There was something mesmerizing in those gray depths, something that held her gaze in his against her will.

Then, suddenly, his eyes softened, dropped lower, and a crooked smile quirked at the corners of his wide, thin mouth. All at once it dawned on her that she was still dressed only in a very flimsy, very revealing, white robe.

Flushing deeply, she crossed her arms over her chest, whirled around and stalked out the door. Behind her, she could hear his low chuckle following her all the way down the hall as she made straight for the telephone. "Humanity be damned!" she repeated, muttering to herself as she dialed Timothy's number. This was her house, he was in her bed, and she'd do what she pleased.

"Oh, Timothy," she cried, virtually sobbing with relief when she heard the familiar, comforting voice. "Can you get out to my place right away?"

"Sarah?" he said, his voice raised in alarm. "What is it? Are you hurt?"

"No, it's not me," she replied impatiently. "A tree fell on this man's car in the storm yesterday, and I had to take him in. I have no idea how badly he's hurt, but he—"

"Hey now, calm down, Sarah. Take a deep breath, then start over again. I take it you have an injured man on your hands. What are his symptoms?"

She did as he told her, breathing deeply in and out a few times, then went on more calmly. "He has a nasty cut on his forehead that I'm afraid could be infected. I'm sure he had a fever last night, but it does seem to have passed this morning. He thinks some ribs might be broken, and he could have concussion."

"You say his fever seems to be down?"

"Well, I haven't taken his temperature, but it seems to be normal. At least he's not still burning up."

"Is he awake? Eating anything?"

"Yes. He seems to be fairly alert, and I just took him in a light breakfast."

"Well, I'll tell you, Sarah. The roads seem to be blocked both ways going out of town. Several trees came down yesterday, and I'm pretty much stuck where I am until the road crews can get them cleared away. We could send a helicopter or a Coast Guard boat if you think the man's condition is serious, but they're all quite busy clearing up after the storm."

"Yes, of course, but that's why I'm calling you, Timothy," Sarah broke in, exasperated. "I don't *know* if his condition is serious, do I? I'm not a doctor after all."

"Well, from what you've told me, it doesn't sound like it. I think he just needs to rest. If a tree fell on his car, knocking him out, he was probably in shock. But so long as he seems alert and is taking nourishment, I don't think you have anything to worry about, at least as far as his physical condition is concerned." Then his voice took on a sober, more pedantic tone. "However, I'm not sure I like the idea of your harboring a strange man."

"Oh, Timothy, he's harmless. He can hardly stay upright for more than a few minutes at a time."

"Still and all, as soon as he's stronger, I think you should insist—"

The line went suddenly dead. At the same moment, Sarah heard a crashing noise coming from the direction of the kitchen, then an ominous silence. The kitchen? she thought wildly. What was he doing in the kitchen?

Slamming the receiver back down, she ran to the kitchen, but there was no one in sight. Then, from the adjoining utility room, she heard a low moaning. Dashing to the door, she peered inside, her heart pounding within her, to see Ross lying there, half-dressed, in a heap on the floor.

CHAPTER TWO

HE HAD obviously made his way there to retrieve
his clothes, where she remembered telling him she'd
hung them out to dry. He'd managed to pull on his
trousers, but that was all.

She stood in the doorway for a few seconds
staring down at him, her heart in her throat, wondering what to do and cursing the fool man. Was
he trying to kill himself?

Then she heard him groan softly. She stirred
herself and knelt down beside him and touched his
bare shoulder.

"Ross," she called softly, shaking him a little.
Then, when he didn't respond, she put her mouth
close to his ear and raised her voice. "Ross. Can
you hear me?"

"Of course I can hear you," he muttered angrily.
"How could I help it when you're shouting in my
ear?" He raised his head and held it in his hands.
"You damn near broke my eardrum."

She gritted her teeth and bit back a sharp retort.
"Well, I'm sorry! I was afraid you'd passed out
again. What happened? And what in the world were
you trying to do?"

"I tripped on that damned hose, that's what
happened." He pointed dramatically down at the
hose she'd retrieved from the garden yesterday when
she was clearing up for the storm.

When she saw him start to struggle to his feet, she reached out for him. "Here, let me help you."

"Never mind," he grumbled. "I can do it myself."

"Very well," she replied in a tight voice. "Have it your way. Far be it from me to interfere."

She stood back from him, arms crossed in front of her and watched him as he struggled to his feet, vowing not to lift a finger to help him. He finally made it, hanging on to the washtub for support, and stood there for a moment, breathing heavily from the exertion, his head bent, his chest heaving.

"What on earth possessed you to get out of bed and come poking around here behind my back in the first place?" she demanded hotly.

He lifted his head and gave her a venomous look. "Behind your back!" he shouted with a dramatic wave of his hand. "What about you? I heard you calling your doctor friend behind *my* back. I knew you would. You're just the type. Can't leave well enough alone, take a man at his word. I told you I didn't want—or need—a doctor."

Sarah's mouth fell open. "Well, of all the ungrateful…" Words failed her. She could only stand there, hands on her hips, spluttering.

Then she saw him start to sway. All the color drained out of his face, his eyes glazed over, and his hand gripped the edge of the washtub so tightly his knuckles were white. Sarah stared at him, appalled. If he fell now, knocked himself unconscious, what could she do?

Suddenly, it was all too much for Sarah, her father's recent death, her confusion about her future, the storm, the accident, and now this pigheaded, bad-tempered man—this *interloper*—who wouldn't stay in bed where he belonged, spied on her telephone calls and refused to see a doctor.

She just couldn't deal with it. With a long, low wail, she covered her face with her hands and burst into loud sobbing. All the tears she hadn't shed during her father's illness or at his funeral came gushing out in an uncontrollable flood from what seemed like a bottomless well of helpless grief.

After a time, she dimly heard someone call her name as though from a great distance, quite low at first, then louder, until finally she couldn't ignore it. With one last shuddering sigh, she blinked her streaming eyes open to see Ross staring at her, still grasping the edge of the washtub, one hand raised toward her.

"Sarah?" he said again. "Are you all right?"

"Oh, of course I'm all right," she snapped.

She sniffled loudly and turned away from him, reaching in the pocket of her robe for a tissue. After mopping her wet face and blowing her nose, she found she was feeling oddly relieved after her outburst, but also more than a little embarrassed by it.

She couldn't even begin to imagine what she must look like, didn't even want to think about it. Not that it made any difference. Who cared what Ross Kirk thought?

"Listen, Sarah," she heard him say behind her in a calm, reasonable tone. "I know I've behaved like a pig, and believe me, I really do appreciate all you've done for me. It's just that it drives me wild to be so helpless. There are things I should be doing, places I need to go."

She turned around slowly to face him again and gave him a wary look. What was he trying to do now? Soft-soap her into something diabolical, no doubt. She didn't trust him an inch. She must have been out of her mind ever to take him inside her house in the first place. She should have left him out in the car and let him fend for himself, if that's what he wanted.

She thought about Timothy's warning. Maybe she should have been more cautious. She knew nothing at all about him. Yet, in spite of his rude behavior, plus the fact that he was a total stranger to her, she had never for a moment really feared he'd do her harm, and she had to wonder why.

She looked at him now, the dark hair mussed, sticking out in all directions and falling over his forehead, the unshaven face, the bare feet and half-fastened, rumpled trousers, the smooth, naked, muscled chest, the bandage on his forehead, filthy by this time. He did look dangerous, even menacing, but not in the way Timothy meant.

Then she caught the expression on his face and looked into his eyes, still a little bloodshot from the accident, but otherwise a clear, deep gray. She couldn't put a name to what she saw there, but something about that calm, confident gaze awakened a response in her that she knew he must feel, too.

As though reading her thoughts, he began to speak in a low, reassuring voice. "I realize, as well, the risk you've taken allowing a strange man into your house. And you're absolutely right that I shouldn't try to move around too much just yet, but I really don't need a doctor." He gave her a disarming smile. "I have a brother who's a doctor, and I've picked up enough from him to know that while I probably do need rest for the moment, my condition is far from critical. So, if you'll just let me stay here another day or two, I'll be on my way. All right?"

She bit her lip and glanced away from that hypnotic gray gaze for a few moments, mulling over his little speech, all the while uncomfortably aware that his eyes never left her face. Then she gave him another dubious look.

What he'd said sounded plausible enough. He didn't strike her as actually a potential danger, yet she still had the feeling she was being set up in some way, conned, used for purposes of his own. But what could she do? It looked as though she was stuck with him, just out of common decency.

"I—I guess so," she replied at last.

"Great. Thank you. And I'll be happy to pay you," he put in hurriedly, as though afraid she might change her mind.

"That won't be necessary," she replied stiffly.

"Whatever," he said. "It's your call." He lifted his broad shoulders in a shrug and immediately started to sway again. "Now, if you'll give me a little help getting back to bed, I think I'm about ready to conk out again."

For the next few days, after that last little scene, there seemed to be a peaceful interlude in their relationship, rather like an armed truce. They treated each other with elaborate courtesy when they had to interact, which was almost exclusively at meals, but for the most part managed to stay out of each other's way.

What Sarah wanted most of all was for him to leave. His presence in the house made her uneasy, especially as he grew stronger, and she thought often of Timothy's warning about taking in a strange man. Still, she didn't feel she could turn him out just yet, not until he was completely recovered from his injuries, and she welcomed each sign of improvement.

Besides, how could he leave? The road crews still hadn't made it up this far to clear the trees and debris that had fallen in the storm, and the heavy branch still lay where it had fallen across the roof of his car. Nor was it possible for anyone to come from the village yet to get him.

He did seem to be gaining in strength each day, or at least he wasn't getting worse, and as he improved physically, his mood seemed to worsen proportionally. Actually, he seemed as anxious to leave as she was to have him gone.

By the third day, he was out of bed and dressed, able to get around on his own, and his sullen, silent presence had begun to get on her nerves as he prowled restlessly around the house, stopping to glare out the window at his immobilized car, his hands stuffed in the pockets of his trousers, his face still haggard and unshaven.

Sarah spent most of her time cleaning up after the storm. Or rather, trying to. She did what she could, but there were several fallen branches she wasn't able to budge, no matter how hard she tried.

By the end of that day, she was about ready to explode herself. She'd spent the entire afternoon cutting and sawing the smaller, more manageable branches off a huge cedar tree that blocked the doorway to the small outbuilding where her father had done most of his paperwork, cataloguing his findings, organizing his material, and writing his reports to the university and the U.S. Wildlife Service. He'd even slept there when he was involved in one of his nighttime projects, and all his records were inside. She needed to retrieve them to get on with her work.

However, even after she'd stripped off every lateral branch, the huge trunk was still immovable. Her hands were numb, every muscle in her body ached, and when it started raining, a fine, sleety, ice-cold onslaught that felt like needles piercing the skin of her face, she finally gave up in despair.

She trudged gloomily back to the house, her face red from the cold, her hair dripping wet, her hands raw from her struggles with the tree. As she approached the house, she noticed a thin wreath of smoke wafting up from the chimney, and when she stepped inside the back door and sniffed the air, she could smell the distinct odor of wood smoke.

Quickly, she stripped off her wet scarf and jacket, slipped her feet out of her muddy boots, then padded softly through the kitchen into the hall and across to the living room. At the doorway, she stood stock-still and stared, the sight that greeted her filling her with a sudden rush of fury.

There he was—that *man*! that *interloper*!— lounging back in her father's chair beside a roaring fire, his legs propped up on the low table in front of it, a glass in his hand, leafing through an old professional journal.

"Enjoying yourself?" she asked in a tight voice.

He looked up, gave her a pleasant smile, and held up the journal. "This is very interesting," he said in a conversational tone. "It seems your father was quite an expert on the migration of whales." Then he frowned. "Is something wrong?"

"Wrong?" she inquired airily. "What could possibly be wrong?" She gave him a grim look. "Except that I half killed myself trying to move one of the trees that came down in the storm and made absolutely no headway. Not to mention the fact that I got soaked to the skin and chilled to the bone out in that freezing rain. But other than that everything's just great."

As the gray eyes flicked over her, a slow smile started to spread across his features, and he chuckled deep in his throat. "Well, I must say you do look a little like a drowned rat."

She glared at him. "So would you if you'd been out there in that rotten weather for two solid hours trying to do the impossible instead of lolling around in here in front of a toasty fire drinking my father's Scotch."

His face clouded over and he narrowed his eyes at her. "And just what's that supposed to mean?"

"Just what it says!" she snapped. "Those felled trees aren't going to clear themselves away, you know. While I've been trying to do a man's work—"

"Hey!" he broke in, raising a hand toward her. "Calm down. It's not my fault, is it? *I* didn't create that storm. *I* didn't ask for that tree to fall on my car. And I'm not exactly thrilled to be here at all. And don't forget, I *am* the injured party here."

Her mouth fell open. "I suppose now it's all *my* fault."

"No, but that tree did grow on your property."

"Well, I can't be held responsible for that. It was an act of God, at least according to my insurance policy."

"Oh, well, if you're going to get technical..." He gave her a swift, appraising glance. "Look, there's no point squabbling like this over something neither one of us could help." Once again, a smile twitched at the corners of his mouth. "And you really do look like something the cat dragged in. I'll tell you what. Why don't you go take a nice hot bath, get on some dry clothes, then come back in front of the fire and I'll fix you a drink. Since we seem to be stuck here alone for the time being, we could at least carry on a civilized conversation, discuss world affairs, maybe even get to know each other a little better."

She eyed him carefully. His words were plausible enough, but something about that smile bothered her. Was he laughing at her? Playing with her? But he was right about one thing. She must look like a total disaster.

Finally, stifling her irritation, she gave him a withering look. "I think I already know you as well as I care to," she pronounced loftily. "Now, if you'll excuse me, I think I will go clean up."

She turned on her heel and walked away from him, slowly and sedately, her head held high. All the while, she had the uncomfortable feeling that those gimlet eyes were fastened on her, the wicked, knowing smile still on his lips.

*   *   *

By the time she'd soaked for half an hour in a hot tub and dressed in clean clothes, all the anger had drained out of her. She had to admit she'd probably behaved childishly, unreasonably. It was a sticky situation for both of them, and none of it was his fault. She'd just been so frustrated at her inability to move that tree that she'd taken in out on him.

As she ran a comb through her still-damp hair, she realized she was rather looking forward to that drink and a good talk. She actually knew very little about him. All she'd found out so far was his name and what his driving license had told her. What kind of work did he do? Was he married? Did he have a family?

For some reason she had the distinct impression he was running from something, and was curious as to what it might be. Nothing criminal, she was certain. He seemed quite respectable, well-spoken. His clothes were good, and he drove an expensive car. The only jewelry he wore was a thin gold watch, but it was obviously a pricey one.

She gave herself one last glance in the mirror before going back to join him. Not exactly a raving beauty, she knew, but her golden hair shone, falling in thick waves to her shoulders, and the cherry red silk shirt set off her dark brown eyes nicely.

When she arrived back in the living room, he was still there, sitting in front of the fire, just as she'd left him. She stopped and stood in the doorway for a moment, studying him. He was lounging back on the sofa, drink in hand, long legs stretched out before him, staring into the flickering fire, his face intent, as though deliberating a thorny problem.

Suddenly, his gaze darted toward her. Their eyes met and held for several long seconds, and for the life of her she couldn't make herself look away. Then, a lazy smile appeared on his face, a peculiar glint in the gray eyes, and his glance swept downward. For a moment, she had the panicky feeling that she'd forgotten to button the clinging red blouse, and it was all she could do to keep from checking to make sure.

Finally, taking a deep breath, she walked slowly over to stand before him and cleared her throat. "Listen, I'm sorry I exploded like that. It's just that I wore myself out trying to move that blasted tree, and I'm afraid when I saw you sitting in here so cozy and comfortable, I just lost it for a minute."

He gave her a searching look, then slowly rose to his feet and gave her a slow smile. "Well, why didn't you just tell me that in the first place? I'm bored out of my mind now that I'm feeling better. I'd gladly welcome something constructive to do, and might even have been able to help you."

They both remained perfectly still for a few moments, just staring silently at each other. Finally, Sarah's gaze fell. There was something very unsettling about that steady scrutiny, and for the first time she noticed just how brilliantly the deep gray eyes gleamed against his tanned face.

"Well," she said, "maybe you can help me tomorrow. That is, if you feel up to it. I really do need to get that tree moved."

"Tell me," he said musingly, "just why is that particular tree so all-fired important?"

"Oh, it's blocking the way to my father's studio," she explained. "I can't get on with my work until I get inside. All my father's records are filed there."

"Records?"

"Yes. You see, my father was a marine biologist, and since his death I've been trying to finish up the project he was working on before he died." She laughed shortly. "Believe me, it's been uphill every step of the way, and it really is urgent that I get at those records as soon as possible to add to them. Now that the wind has died down, the wildlife population around here will be pretty active."

"It's that important to you, then? That you finish his project?"

"Well, yes, it is. My father lived for his work here. I've helped him ever since I was a child, especially after my mother died."

"And was she a marine biologist, too?"

Sarah nodded. "Yes. In fact, they were quite a well-known team, even prominent in their field."

"And you took your mother's place when she died, I gather."

Sarah eyed him narrowly. "As a matter of fact, yes. But you make it sound like some deep Freudian mystery."

"Not at all," he assured her hastily. "And I'd be happy to try to help you get that tree moved tomorrow."

"Great. Now, how about that drink you promised me?"

"Right," he said and walked over to the credenza against the far wall where her father had kept his meager supply of liquor. "This Scotch isn't bad," he said, raising a bottle. "How about it?"

"That would be fine."

Watching him as he deftly poured out her drink, it was almost as though she were seeing him for the first time, and she had to admit he was a very good-looking man, even handsome. Then she had to smile. Or he would be except for the three days' growth of black stubble on his square jaw, his hair a little too long and falling over his forehead. Nor did the wrinkled shirt and dark trousers improve his image. They had been through the washing machine, but weren't pressed.

She wondered idly how he would look shaven and with some decent clothes. He had fine eyes, a firm chin and a strong, straight nose. The planes of his face hollowed down from rather prominent cheekbones, and when he smiled two clefts appeared at the sides of his thin mouth.

She didn't realize she was staring at him until his voice broke the stillness. "Well?"

"What?"

"I asked you if you wanted water or soda."

"Oh, I don't care. Water, I guess."

He splashed some water in her glass from the pitcher, then came back to hand it to her. "Where were you a minute ago? Woolgathering?"

She laughed nervously. "I was just thinking. You could probably stand a little grooming yourself." She thought a minute. "I gave away most of my father's personal effects and clothing when he died, but he did keep a shaving kit and some clean shirts and trousers in the studio. If we can get that tree blocking the door moved tomorrow, I'll find them for you." She put a hand under her chin and squinted narrowly at him. "He was a tall man, too.

Not as big as you are, I don't think, but we should be able to come up with something that will fit you."

"Sounds great," he replied with a broad grin. "Although if I can get into my car, I have a suitcase in there." Then the smile faded and his voice softened. "I take it your father died only recently."

"Yes," she said shortly. "Just six months ago."

"And you still miss him."

"Yes." Even now, she could feel the tears sting behind her eyes at the memory.

"How did he die?"

"A heart attack. Very sudden. In fact, he was in his studio working when it happened."

"Then he didn't suffer. And he was able to do the work he loved right to the end. That's something to be grateful for."

"Oh, yes. I am," she said softly.

He reached for the journal he'd been reading earlier and held it out, turning to an article her father had written. "His work sounds very interesting. You must have been a big help to him."

She nodded. "Yes, I think so. And I found it as fascinating as he did."

"Will you try to continue now that he's gone?"

"I'm not sure," she said slowly. "I love the work, but I'm afraid I won't be able to keep up with it on my own. My father was the real expert and quite highly regarded in his field. He had the reputation, the connections, and I doubt any work I did on my own would be accepted by the scientific community."

"Yes, I can see how that might be a problem. Sounds as though you plan to give it up when you finish that last project you mentioned."

She shrugged. "I'm afraid I'll have to."

"Tell me more about what it is exactly that you do," he said. He pointed at a photograph in the journal. "These birds, for instance."

"Oh, those are cormorants."

"Not whales," he said with a smile.

"Well, although we do track the migration patterns of some shorebirds, our main area of study is sea mammals, like otters, seals, porpoises and gray whales in particular. They're the most interesting, probably because they're the largest species we have around here; some of them up to forty feet long."

He gave a low whistle. "That's a pretty big animal. Are they dangerous?"

She laughed. "Heavens, no! They're very gentle, playful creatures. Of course, they could capsize a fishing boat if they came too close, so the fishermen in these parts know enough to give them a wide berth. But they aren't even meat-eaters. They subsist mostly on plankton. It's the Orcas that prey on fish and smaller mammals."

"What are you looking for in your study?"

"Mostly their migration habits. The whole subject of why birds and animals migrate is still pretty much of a mystery. We know the gray whales go north from California to Alaska in the spring to the Arctic breeding grounds, then travel back down south in the autumn, but no one is really sure why. They travel in pods, you see, anywhere from four to five to forty of them, whole families—"

She broke off abruptly, suddenly aware that she'd been babbling, warming to her favorite subject, and that Ross was staring intently at her.

"But this must all be very boring to you," she said with a nervous laugh. "I'm afraid I tend to get carried away."

"Not at all," he assured her firmly. "It sounds fascinating. And I'm impressed with your expertise, your dedication. What I don't understand is why you think you can't do it alone."

"Well, I explained that. It was my father—"

"Wait!" he broke in, holding up a hand. "Just hold on a minute here. I know you loved and admired your father, and I respect that, but as great a man as he might have been, surely you contributed more to his work than transcribing his notes."

"Well, yes, but he had all the credentials. I don't even have a degree."

"Why not?"

She gave him a puzzled look. "I didn't really need one," she replied slowly. "At least while my father was alive. Although I did start university when I finished high school. I had about three years of study toward a degree when my mother died. He needed my help then to continue his work, and I saw no reason to go on with my education."

"What's to stop you from getting one now?"

She stared blankly at him. "I don't know. It's rather late in the day for that, isn't it?"

"Listen, Sarah," he said, leaning toward her. "You didn't die with your father. You sound as though your life, your work, ended when his did. There's nothing in the whole wide world stopping you from finishing up your degree. If you want it badly enough, that is. There's always a way." He thought a moment, chin in hand. "Is it a question of money? If so, I have some connections who might be able to help with a scholarship, or perhaps even a grant of some kind. After all, you're not exactly a rank amateur in the field."

She gave a vigorous shake of her head. "Oh, no. My father left me well provided for. I mean, I'm not rich by any means, but I have enough to get by." A sudden surge of excitement, of real hope, began to spread through her and she gazed up at him now, her eyes flashing. "Ross, do you really think I could?"

"Absolutely."

Then, suddenly, the color drained from his face, and he put a hand to his head.

"Ross, what is it?" she said, startled.

"I'm not sure," came the faint reply. He raised his head and gave her a weak smile. "But I think it might be a good idea to get back in that bed."

"Here," she said, reaching out to him. "Let me help you."

She put an arm around his waist, and with him leaning heavily against her, his hand clutching her shoulder, they made their way slowly down the hall to his bedroom. She guided him over to the bed, and he sank down on it with a sigh.

"Will you be all right?" she asked anxiously. "I mean, can you manage to get into bed on your own?"

He raised his eyes and gave her a dazed look. "I'm not sure. Maybe if you could just help me with my shirt."

She knelt down before him, then reached out and began to undo the buttons of his shirt, her heart pounding, her fingers fumbling. What if he had a relapse? Became unconscious?

When all the buttons were finally unfastened, she tugged the shirt down over his shoulders and arms. He sat perfectly still throughout her ministrations. The only sound in the room was his own steady breathing and the wild beating of her own heart, thundering in her ears.

Beyond her fears for his physical state, she gradually became aware of something else, an unfamiliar feeling, a slow warmth that seemed to be heating up by the second as her hands made contact with the bare flesh beneath the shirt.

Quickly, she dropped it down on the bed beside him and jumped to her feet. "There," she said. "You can handle the rest yourself, can't you?"

"I suppose so," came the distant reply.

It was quite dark in the room, with only the hall light to illuminate it. His face was in the shadows, but as she gazed down at him, she could have sworn there was a glint in those gray eyes that belied the dazed weakness he'd shown earlier.

She backed away a step. "I'll say good-night, then. If you need anything, just give a shout."

She hurried down the hall back to the living room. The fire was dying, and she stood there staring down at the burning embers for a long time, her head in a whirl of confusion. Of course he was still probably a little shaky from his injuries, and it was perfectly understandable that he would tire easily, need rest, but she couldn't quite ward off the uneasy feeling that there was more to that sudden attack than physical weakness.

Then she shook herself. She was being silly, reading some significance into what was a perfectly natural reaction to his injuries. It was all her imagination. What was really disturbing her, she suddenly realized, was her own response to those solid-muscled shoulders, that smooth, bare skin.

She thought about their earlier conversation. For such an abrupt, even curt man, clearly short-tempered, he'd been amazingly understanding and gentle about her father's death and quite encouraging about her own future. In fact, it seemed there might be quite a lot more to Ross Kirk than she'd realized at first.

As she trailed slowly into the kitchen to fix herself some dinner, it dawned on her how lonely she'd been since her father died. And how hungry for companionship. She mustn't let that carry her away into something she wouldn't be able to handle.

With luck, Ross would get his strength back soon and be on his way, back to wherever he came from, out of her life. That's what she wanted. Wasn't it?

CHAPTER THREE

EARLY the next morning, Sarah was jolted out of a sound sleep by a sudden explosive clamor coming from outside. She sat bolt upright in bed, still groggy, trying to identify its source.

It sounded very much like a chain saw still some distance away, but shattering in the early-morning stillness. Apparently, the road crew had arrived to clear away the trees and debris that had blown down in the storm.

Her first thought was that it meant Ross would be leaving soon. He could get his car repaired, see a doctor, and her responsibility for him would be at an end. But instead of the rush of gratitude she'd expected, for some reason she found her spirits drooping considerably.

Then, suddenly, the chain saw sputtered and died and the grinding din stopped. Perhaps they wouldn't get up this far for a while after all.

She jumped out of bed and ran to the window. The sea was quite calm today, a pale sun struggling to come out from behind a high bank of fluffy white clouds. But it was still freezing cold, and she dressed quickly in her warmest shirt and heavy sweater.

To her surprise, Ross was in the kitchen when she got there, standing at the stove with his back toward her. The rich aroma of freshly brewed coffee filled the air, and she could hear bacon sizzling in the pan.

She stood in the doorway staring at him for a moment. It was vaguely unsettling to her to see this stranger in her kitchen, a man so tall that the room seemed to be filled with his presence, yet she felt oddly comforted at the same time.

Just then he turned around. "Good morning," he called out cheerily as he came walking toward her, brandishing a spatula in one hand. "I found some bacon and eggs in the fridge and thought I'd surprise you with breakfast." He grinned. "My culinary skills aren't exactly world-class, but I can toss a mean omelet. Sit down. Let me wait on you for a change."

"Sounds great," she said, seating herself at the table and folding her hands on top of it. Then she sniffed the air and pointed at the thick black cloud rising from the frying pan on the stove behind him. "But I think you'd better tend to your business a little more closely," she commented with a smile. "It looks as though at least half your efforts are going up in smoke."

"Oh, drat," he said, pivoting and striding back to the stove. "And I wanted to impress you," he called over his shoulder.

"Oh, you have," she replied, laughing. "Just the fact that you made the effort is quite impressive in itself."

He filled their plates and came back to set them on the table. "Well, let's dig in," he said, taking a seat across from her. "I just hope it's edible at least."

All of a sudden, the buzz of the chain saw started up again, piercing the air. It sounded much closer this time. They both glanced up quickly from their plates, and their eyes met across the table. Then Ross picked up his fork and looked away.

"They've been at it since seven o'clock this morning and it sounds as though they're making their way up here pretty fast. With any luck, you'll probably be rid of me soon."

"Yes," she replied. "I imagine you're anxious to leave."

"Oh, not all that anxious," he replied briefly. "But I think I will take a walk after breakfast to see what kind of progress they're making. That is," he added pointedly, "after I help you move that tree you mentioned last night." He rubbed a hand over his bristly chin. "And if I'm about to reenter the civilized world, I'd better try to improve my image a little. I feel like something that just crawled out from under a rock."

"Does my life here seem so uncivilized to you, then?" she asked. Although she strove for a light tone, her words came out in a tight voice and more defensively than she'd intended.

His eyes widened in consternation. "Oh, Lord, no! That's not what I meant at all." He leaned across the table toward her, his face concerned. "In fact, I rather envy you your situation. It seems so simple, so uncomplicated, compared to mine." He sighed and sank back in his chair. "You have no idea the kind of circus I left behind, or how peaceful these past few days have seemed to me."

"Just what is your life, Ross?" she asked carefully. She laughed lightly. "You've learned quite a bit about mine, what there is of it, since you've been here, but I don't know anything about you, your family, your work. You call it a circus. That sounds a little harrowing, but it must be exciting.''

He waved his fork in the air dismissively. ''Oh, just because I think it's complex doesn't mean it's interesting. As a matter of fact, one of the reasons I took this trip alone was to sort out a few things, personal things, that had begun to build up.''

He gazed off into the distance for a few moments, and she waited, hoping he would tell her what those personal things might be, but when he turned back to her he was smiling wryly.

''As for the bare facts, however, my home is in San Francisco. I have a rather exalted position with a family business that deals in various enterprises, such as real-estate holdings, stocks and bonds.'' He shrugged. ''We own a few small electronics companies and dabble in commodities futures. It sounds a lot grander than it is, and as I said, boring as hell.''

She laced her fingers under her chin and gave him a narrow look. ''Boring in what way?'' she asked. ''It sounds fascinating—and very important.''

''Oh, not really. It's a rat race. What is there left to do when money is not a problem and the work is repetitive, handled mostly by other people anyway?'' He pushed his chair back. ''And speaking of money, before I leave, you must let me repay you in some way for your hospitality. You know, you probably saved my life.'' He laid a finger lightly over the bandage on his forehead. ''If you hadn't come along to drag me out of that car and take care of this, there's no telling what would have become of me.''

"I didn't do anything anyone wouldn't have," she replied firmly. "And I won't even discuss payment of any kind." She grinned. "If you can help me get that tree moved this morning, that would be ample payment. As I mentioned last night, I can't get on with my project until I get into that studio, and autumn is one of the busiest times of the year for migrating wildlife."

He gave her a long, close look, chewing thoughtfully. "You make it sound..." He broke off, frowned, then shrugged. "I don't know, somehow terribly urgent. Don't you think you might be a little obsessive about finishing your father's project? I mean, is your work—your *father's* work, actually," he added pointedly, "all you ever think about?"

She gazed at him, appalled, stung by the accusation in his words, ready to lash out at him, defend herself. Then she saw the gleam in the gray eyes, the way his mouth twitched at the corners. He was baiting her again! Trying to get a rise out of her. Well, she wouldn't give him the satisfaction.

Instead, she gave him a cool smile. "Is that how it sounds to you?" she asked.

He shrugged. "Well, I just have to wonder why a young woman like you—intelligent, attractive, capable—would want to bury herself in this godforsaken place just to fill the shoes of her dead parents."

Sarah gave him a withering look. "You don't know what you're talking about," she stated icily. "And, I might add, you're very quick to pry into other people's motives and make superficial snap judgments about them for a man who doesn't appear to be managing his own life so wonderfully."

His face hardened. "You know nothing about my life," he said in a flat, toneless voice.

"Exactly my point," she snapped.

She set down her fork, dabbed her mouth carefully with her napkin, and rose from the table. She gave him one last saccharine smile, then turned on her heel and stalked slowly, sedately, out of the room.

It wasn't until she had reached the sanctuary of her own bedroom that her heartbeat slowed, her hands stopped shaking. His penetrating assessment of her situation had disturbed her deeply, hit too close to the bone for comfort.

She knew quite well that the life she had lived here with her father, so isolated from normal society, so totally dedicated to his work, was unnatural, certainly not a normal way for a young woman to live. But she had been devoted to both her parents, to the seashore wildlife they studied, and for the most part she had been content, had even guarded her privacy jealously.

Now, suddenly, she began to wonder if she hadn't missed something—some critical aspect of normal life—and all because this strange man had entered her world so unexpectedly. Thank God he'd be leaving soon! In time she'd forget he'd ever been here.

Just then the telephone rang, and she went into the hall to answer it. It was Timothy.

"How are you doing up there?" came his cheery voice.

"Oh, hello, Timothy. I'm doing fine. Still trying to clear away the debris from the storm."

"I meant to call you sooner, but you can imagine how busy I've been. There were quite a lot of injuries, and our sad excuse for a hospital here in the village is chock-full of broken bones and bruises."

"I understand. Don't give it another thought. We've been managing just fine."

"So, how's your patient?"

"He seems much better. In fact, he's going to help me move a tree today that's blocking the doorway to my father's studio."

"Oh, better not just yet, Sarah," he said hastily. "If he has cracked ribs, he could easily puncture a lung with any undue physical exertion."

"You're right, of course," she said. "I hadn't even thought of that."

"Furthermore, if he did have concussion, he definitely should rest a few days more. Better keep him down for a while longer, at least until I can take a look at him."

"Of course. Anything you say. You're the doctor." She paused. "I heard the road crew out working this morning with their chain saw, but have no idea when they'll make it to my place."

"Oh, it won't be long now. They've already cleared up the main roads around the village. Tell you what, I'll take a drive up your way this afternoon when I finish my rounds at the hospital, see if I can get through by then. If so, I'll give him a good going-over."

"Thanks, Timothy. I'd appreciate that."

"See you then."

When they'd hung up, Sarah had a moment's doubt about the wisdom of encouraging Timothy's visit. Ross had been pretty adamant about not wanting a doctor.

Well, that was just too bad! If he was still not quite out of the woods, she didn't want to be responsible for him if he got worse. And if the workmen did get this far today, she could ask them to clear away the tree.

Bracing herself to confront Ross with her decision, she marched purposefully down the hall to the kitchen. But when she got there, he was gone. The breakfast dishes had been washed and dried, all the food cleared away, and the room looked neat and tidy.

She walked back to his bedroom, but there was no sign of him there, either. In fact, the house was utterly silent, and panic suddenly clutched at her heart. Could he have gone out back to try to move that tree all by himself?

He wouldn't! He just didn't strike her as the kind of man who would need to prove his macho masculinity by such a foolhardy move. From the little she knew about him, he had his share of male ego, but it seemed to come from an authentic, unshakable self-confidence. In fact, he struck her as the kind of man who pretty much went his own way, and certainly would never feel the need to prove anything.

Still, you never could tell. She'd only known him a few days, and even that short acquaintance had been conducted under unusual circumstances. He'd actually been unconscious for part of that time, and most of her conclusions about him were sheer guesswork.

She raced to the door, flung it open and was about to dart around the house to the studio when she saw him coming up the path from the road. Breathing a sigh of relief, she stood there waiting for him, watching him. He was carrying a worn leather suitcase in one hand, a matching briefcase in the other, and he certainly looked fit enough. His stride was firm, he held himself erect, and when he saw her he gave her a broad grin.

"Don't worry," he called out to her as he came up the path toward her. "I'm not moving in permanently."

Yet, when she got a closer look at him, she could see the beads of perspiration gleaming on his forehead, hear his rapid, rasping breathing, all on a cold day and from very little exertion, and her decision to insist that he wait until Timothy examined him before trying to do anything strenuous was only confirmed.

He set the cases down. "I'd forgotten these were in the car." He tapped his forehead lightly. "Must be the blow to the head. Anyway," he went on, "it looks like they're almost through clearing the road, and I thought I'd like a change of clothes before I leave." He glanced down at the wrinkled plaid shirt, the dark trousers he'd been living in for the past several days. "That is," he added, "if I can get someone to come and tow the car away and make some repairs."

"Did you try it, then?" she asked as they went back inside.

He nodded. "I'm no mechanic, but I think the problem is simple enough—just a matter of getting it up on a hoist and checking the underside. Something seems to be jammed, but I don't think it's serious." He gave her a sideways glance. "That is, if your village has such a thing as a mechanic."

"Oh, yes. Quite a good one, as a matter of fact. We're not entirely primitive here, you know." She took a deep breath. "But as far as your leaving goes, I'd like to have you wait until later today."

"Don't worry," he assured her quickly. "I intend to help you with that tree before I go." Then his voice lowered, took on a more serious note. "It's the least I can do after all you've done for me."

"Oh, I don't know about that," she rejoined lightly. "But that wasn't what I meant. I talked to Timothy, my doctor friend, this morning, and he was adamant that you shouldn't try to do anything strenuous until he examines you."

"Nonsense!" he exploded. "Utter nonsense!"

"No, Ross, it's not. He said you could puncture a lung with a cracked rib, and that after concussion you need a lot more rest than you've had so far."

He opened his mouth, obviously about to protest, then snapped it shut and fixed her with an inquiring look. "Just who is this Timothy of yours anyway? How old is he?"

"I told you. He's the local doctor. And I have no idea how old he is. Around your age, I'd say. What difference does it make? Do you have some hang-up about the age of your doctor?"

"And he's a good friend?"

"Well, yes. I've known him for years."

"How good a friend?"

From the knowing look on his lean face and the rather smug smile that quirked at the corners of his mouth, she knew quite well what he was implying, and to her dismay felt her face go up in flame.

"That's my business, isn't it?" she snapped, turning her head away to hide her confusion.

But it was too late for that. Those gimlet gray eyes of his seemed to be able to penetrate far beyond her feeble attempts to cover her embarrassing reaction.

"Aha," he drawled. "So that's how it is."

"I don't know what you're talking about. Nor do you, either, I might add."

"Why so defensive?" he asked smoothly. "There's nothing to be ashamed of, is there? I mean, is the guy married?"

"No."

"Well, then?" When she didn't reply, he plowed inexorably on. "Maybe you worship him from afar and he—"

She stamped her foot, cutting him off. "That's enough!" she cried. "What I feel for Timothy or he feels for me is not your affair. Now, are you going to let him examine you or not? I don't care one way or the other. Every bone in your body could be broken, including that thick skull, and it wouldn't matter to me." She paused dramatically, crossing her arms over her heaving chest and glared at him. "Well?"

His eyes had widened perceptibly throughout her harangue. Now he only nodded. "Yes," he said. "I will."

Her mouth fell open. "You will?"

"Yes. It's probably a good idea. And, listen, Sarah, I probably shouldn't have teased you that way. It's a nasty habit of mine. I have two younger sisters who were the bane of my existence while we were growing up, real little brats, and somehow you remind me of them, one in particular." He chuckled reminiscently. "As it turned out, I'm probably closer to her now than any other member of my family."

Somewhat mollified, Sarah gave him a thin smile. "Well, I guess I didn't need to lose my temper like that, either," she admitted grudgingly. Then she laughed. "I'm afraid as an only child, with rather elderly parents, I'm not used to the rough-and-tumble of family life." His remark about his younger sisters intrigued her. "Tell me, do you have other brothers and sisters?"

His face shut down. "An older brother," he said in a clipped voice. "But that's a dull subject. Now, shall we at least go take a look at that tree of yours? It may not be as immovable as you believe."

"I don't think so," she said. She grabbed her heavy jacket off the chair where she'd set it down and began to shrug into it. "Let's wait until Timothy has a look at you. Besides, I want to take a walk up the beach to check on a neighbor of mine, see how she weathered the storm or if she needs any help. She lives alone and is getting on in years. I tried to call her a couple of times and she didn't answer."

"That sounds like a good idea," he said. "Why don't I go with you? I could stand a little exercise after being cooped up here for so long."

"No!" she replied hastily.

The last thing she needed was to have her neighbor find out Ross had been staying with her. Carol was basically a good-hearted soul, had been one of her dead mother's closest friends, but was an inveterate gossip. If she knew about Ross, by that afternoon it would be common knowledge in the whole village. She definitely didn't need that kind of speculation about her private life.

Then she noticed the strange look Ross was giving her, almost as though she'd hurt his feelings. "I really don't think that would be a good idea," she added in a softer tone.

"What's the matter?" he said. "Are you ashamed of me?" Then a light seemed to dawn and a slow smile spread across his face. "Ah, I have it. You don't want the neighbors gossiping about you. Is that it?"

"Well, partly," she had to admit. "Besides, Timothy seems to think you need rest more than anything else. Why don't you go lie down? Then we can have some lunch when I get back."

He nodded absently. "I just might do that," he said. "Have a good walk. And I hope your neighbor is all right."

Although the sun was shining, a brisk, chill breeze had come up, raising whitecaps on the ocean and bending the tall trees along the shore. Sarah walked against the wind, her head bent, her hands stuffed in the pockets of her jacket, still irritated by Ross's comments, especially his insinuations about Timothy.

Ross Kirk could be a maddening man, but not a cruel one. He didn't mean any real harm. She just wasn't used to that kind of teasing and had probably overreacted. And she *was* oversensitive about Timothy. In fact, she rather wished now she'd told Ross the truth, that far from her worshiping Timothy from afar, he'd asked her to marry him after her father died. It wouldn't hurt Ross to realize that a decent, good-looking man loved her, desired her, especially after he'd compared her to his sister.

His sister! Is that all he thought of her? Images of him rose up in her mind. Lying half-comatose in bed, his lithe, athletic body outlined under the covers, the bare chest and shoulders, the strongly muscled arms...

She'd reached Carol's by now, and just then saw her friend out in the garden struggling with a rose bush that had been blown over in the storm and trying to tie it up securely. She was a short, rather stout gray-haired woman of indeterminate age, but certainly well past her first youth.

"Hi, Carol," Sarah called, going in through the gate.

"Sarah! What a pleasant surprise." Carol stood back and eyed the rose bush. "There," she said with satisfaction. "That should do it." She turned back to Sarah. "Am I glad to see you," she called. "I've been dying for some company."

"Oh, I can't stay," Sarah replied, coming up the path to join her. "I really just came by to check on you and make sure you'd managed all right during the storm."

"That was a beauty, wasn't it?" The older woman pulled off her gloves and gave Sarah a searching look. "Well, at least you can stay long enough to tell me about the man who's been staying at your place."

Sarah could only stare. What did they use? Smoke signals? Tom-toms? ESP?

"How on earth did you find out about that?" she asked.

Carol chuckled. "Oh, my dear, how could I not have found out? His car has been in the road in front of your house for days now. And actually, I saw him myself yesterday when I strolled down your way." Her sharp, beady brown eyes fastened on Sarah. "Why does that bother you?"

"It doesn't, really," Sarah replied quickly. "Of course not. Why should it? I was just surprised, that's all."

"Well, then. Who is he? He looks interesting. A real hunk."

Sarah had to smile. "I guess you could say that," she said.

"I noticed, too, that his head was bandaged. Was he badly hurt? From the looks of that tree lying across his car, I'd say he was lucky still to be alive."

"Yes, he is. In fact, I was terrified the man might die on me. I had no idea what to do with him. And I couldn't just turn him away," she added somewhat defensively.

"No," Carol murmured. "Of course not."

"Anyway, he's quite anxious to leave now that he's feeling better."

"And are you anxious to have him go?"

"As a matter of fact, I am. It's been a real worry having an injured man in the house, not knowing how badly he was hurt. A stranger at that."

"Well, if he was hurt, you probably were never in any real danger from him. What do you know about him?"

Sarah laughed shortly. "Very little, actually. I know his name is Ross Kirk and he lives in San

Francisco, but that's about all. Oh, and he works for a family firm, has two younger sisters and an older brother."

"And that's it?"

Sarah nodded. "Remember, he was half-unconscious most of the time. Now, I really do have to get back. There's an enormous tree blocking the way to the studio, and I want to try to talk the road crew into taking it out for me."

Back at the house, Sarah was surprised to see Timothy's familiar black car in the driveway. They must have gotten the road cleared sooner than she thought.

She hurried her pace and went inside the house. She could hear the low murmur of male voices coming from the kitchen and, shrugging off her jacket, walked toward it.

Ross was sitting on a chair by the window, bare-chested, a fresh tape around his ribs, with Timothy standing before him, bending down to shine a light into his eyes. Both men were turned away from her, and she stood in the doorway for a few moments gazing at them.

It would be hard to imagine two men more dis-similar. Timothy was short and stocky with a rather plump, smooth-shaven face, his sandy hair neatly combed, dressed in a suit and tie. Ross, on the other hand, looked almost like a dangerous rogue in con-trast. He still hadn't shaved and the stubble on his face was as dark as the tousled hair that fell about his head every which way.

There was a lean and hungry look about him as he slouched back in the chair, his long legs spread apart in front of him, his arms hanging loosely at his sides. Yet, he seemed pliable enough. At least he was allowing Timothy to get on with his examination.

"Well, Doctor," she said brightly, stepping into the room. "What's the diagnosis?"

Both men turned to look at her at once, Timothy beaming, his rather cherubic face wreathed in a smile, as though happy to see her, while Ross only glared, narrow-eyed, his arms crossed now over his freshly bandaged chest.

"Well," Timothy said in his cheeriest bedside manner, "he does still have symptoms of concussion, and although I can't be positive without an X ray, there do seem to be a few broken ribs. As you can see, I taped them up more securely. But the head wound looks all right. No infection. And he doesn't have a fever."

"Do you think he's well enough to travel?" she asked.

"Oh, no. I'd say not. He'd better not try to do any driving until his head is more together and those ribs heal."

All of a sudden, Ross leaped from his chair, put his hands on his hips and glared from Sarah to Timothy, then back to Sarah again.

"Will you two please quit talking about me as though I weren't even here?" he demanded loudly. "*I'll* decide whether I'm well enough to travel, if you don't mind."

Timothy only laughed. "Of course, old man," he said with an indulgent smile. "It's entirely up to you. I'm just telling you that if you try to drive you could end piled up in a ditch or flat against a tree. But suit yourself. I've given you my best advice, which is to take it easy for another week or two at least. Then I'll take another look at you.''

As he turned and started packing his instruments away in his black bag, there was a sudden dead, fraught silence in the room. It was as though time had stopped altogether. Finally, Sarah sneaked a look at Ross. He was still glaring at Timothy's bent head, and it was all she could do to suppress the giggles that threatened to erupt at any moment.

Then, ignoring Ross completely, Timothy turned to Sarah. ''I have several other calls to make, so better be on my way. Glad to see you got through the storm all right, Sarah. I'll talk to you later.'' He made for the door. ''Don't bother to see me out. I know the way.''

When he was gone, Sarah turned slowly to face Ross, who was still standing by the window. He didn't look quite so angry now, however, and she gave him a bright smile.

''Well, that's not so bad,'' she said heartily. ''Just a couple of weeks. And at least you know now you don't have anything seriously wrong with you.''

He came walking slowly toward her, and with each step a familiar satanic smile seemed to spread wider on his face. Finally, he stood directly before her, beaming down at her.

''No,'' he said in a pleasant conversational tone, ''two weeks isn't so bad. Of course, since it's all your idea, you won't mind my staying on here with you while I recuperate, will you?''

CHAPTER FOUR

SARAH stared at him, wide-eyed. She hadn't counted on that! For some reason, she'd assumed that since the roads were cleared he'd be leaving, go to the hospital, or at least find a place to stay in the village. To tell the truth, she didn't know *what* she'd thought, only felt relief that he was in no imminent danger.

In the meantime, Ross continued to gaze at her with that same maddening look of the utmost innocence, his gray eyes candid, the same silly smirk on his face, waiting for her reaction. Was he just teasing her, playing with her again, or did he really mean it?

She eyed him suspiciously. "I thought you were so convinced there was nothing wrong with you."

He shrugged. "I may be a somewhat stubborn man, but I'm not stupid. When a qualified doctor tells me I could do myself serious damage, I'm not too pigheaded to pay attention. He's the expert after all."

That made sense, but she still wasn't entirely convinced. He *seemed* serious enough. His expression had grown grave, and he was watching her now with a rather soulful look, as though throwing himself on her mercy.

"You certainly changed your tune in a hurry," she said at last. "Five minutes ago you were hell-

bent on getting out of here at any cost and certainly
didn't seem about to take an expert's advice.''

He flashed her a broad grin. ''Well, who are you
going to believe? Me or that doctor of yours?''

''I *wish* you'd quit referring to him as *my*
doctor!'' she shot back angrily. ''I told you, he's
only a friend.''

''Sorry'' was the offhand reply. ''Well, then?
How about it? Are you going to let me stay on here
until I get a clean bill of health from *my* doctor or
not?''

''I just don't know if that would be such a good
idea,'' she said carefully.

''Why not?'' he asked in an eminently reasonable
tone. ''Still afraid of gossip?''

Well, was she? Not really. There might be some
speculation, but the village people knew her so well
they'd never believe she was carrying on a torrid
affair with an injured man. Besides, even if it did
become food for gossip, it would probably only
make her more interesting to them than the pro-
fessor's quiet and *boring* little daughter. She'd
grown rather sick of that role anyway. Maybe it
was time she broke the mold and took a risk or
two.

What really bothered her and made her hesitate
was a nagging feeling that she'd be letting herself
in over her head if he stayed on. Little warning bells
had already started to clang. Those wayward visions
she'd had of him lying half-naked in bed didn't
come from any burning desire to tend the sick. On
the contrary, his weakness had been far easier to
handle than the strength she now sensed in him,

the power he could wield over her if she gave in to those feelings.

She continued to stand there without speaking, unable to make up her mind which way to jump, biting her lip and staring down at the floor, until finally his voice broke into the dead silence.

"Of course," he said in a brisk, rather distant voice, "I quite understand that you don't want a virtual stranger hanging around now that the real emergency is over. There must be some place I can stay in the village until my car is fixed and Timothy tells me I'm well enough to drive."

Sarah raised her eyes to his, searching her mind. There was no hotel in the village, or even a bed and breakfast, and the closest resort was a good twenty miles down the coast at Ocean Shores. How would he get to the doctor for treatment when he couldn't drive? There must be a taxi service around somewhere, but if there was she'd never heard of it.

"What I was thinking," he went on, "was that I might be able to stay on in your father's studio. That way I wouldn't be underfoot or get in your way. You said he used to stay out there himself, so there must be water, electricity, bathroom facilities and so on."

"Oh, yes," she murmured, weakening. "It's actually quite self-contained. There's a hot plate and a small fridge, even a good supply of canned goods."

As though sensing she was about to give in, he added hurriedly, "It should only be for a couple of weeks or so. And I would insist on paying you."

Should she or shouldn't she? What harm would it do? She could easily retrieve the data she needed from the studio and work on her project in the house. Wasn't it only common decency to let him stay on until he was fully recovered? After all, it had been a tree from her property that had caused all the damage.

"Well, I guess it would be all right," she said slowly. "I do feel some responsibility for what happened to you after all, and to be honest, I can't think of an alternative anyway. There really isn't anywhere else for you to go."

"Great," he said, nodding vigorously, as though afraid she might change her mind.

Then he winced and put a hand to his head. He seemed to sway a little, as though unsteady on his feet. He reached out to clutch at the back of a nearby chair and closed his eyes.

Alarmed, Sarah ran to his side and put a hand on his arm. "Ross, are you all right?"

His eyes blinked open, focused on her, and he gave her a weak smile. "Yes, I think so. Just a little dizzy spell. I think concussion can do that."

"Well, if you feel up to it, let's go out and take a look at the studio. We can get inside now that the road crew has moved that tree. The bed is all made up, and you probably should lie down."

With her arm around his waist guiding him, they made their way slowly out into the yard and down the path to the studio. He seemed amazingly docile, leaning against her. Apparently, Timothy's warnings really had made an impression on him, put the fear of God in him as to just how serious the consequences of his injuries could be.

The studio consisted of one large all-purpose room, with a tiny bathroom behind an alcove.

There was a small bed and dresser along one wall, her father's desk and filing cabinets against another, and off in one corner, a small counter with a sink and hot plate.

Although it was spotlessly clean, it was a little stuffy from being shut up for so long. Since it was such a fine day, Sarah opened the window over the counter to air it out. In the meantime, Ross had made his way to the cot and sat down.

"Well?" she said, turning to him. "What do you think?" She laughed. "It's not exactly the Waldorf-Astoria, but you should find everything you need."

"It'll do nicely," he agreed. "And I do have my own personal things in my suitcase. After I rest awhile, I'll come to the house and pick it up."

For some reason, now that his staying on seemed to be settled, Sarah felt uncomfortable in his presence, even a little embarrassed. To hide her confusion, she turned away from him and began collecting the record books that lay on top of the desk where she'd left them the last time she'd worked out here.

Gathering up an armload of what she'd need right away, she started to leave. At the door, she turned around. He was still sitting in the same position, knees apart, his hands laced between them, gazing at her with a bland expression.

"If you need anything," she said, "just give a yell."

"I'll be fine," he said.

"Well, then..." Her voice trailed off. What more was there to say?

She turned and stepped out into the sunshine, closing the door behind her. As she started walking slowly up the path toward the house, she was already regretting her decision to let him stay. With each step she took, her apprehension grew, so that by the time she reached her door, she was in a state of near panic.

What had possessed her to agree to such a thing? It had all sounded so plausible when *he* was explaining it. Now she felt as though she'd been maneuvered into a sticky situation that could only get worse.

But there really wasn't any other place for him to go. She was in no danger from him. He wasn't a criminal type by any means. Far from it. Besides, now that Carol and Timothy knew he was staying with her, the whole village would find out, so that even if he did have any evil intentions, he wouldn't dare go through with them.

Well, it was done now. If he became a nuisance, she'd just have to be firm with him, explain to him how important it was to her to finish her father's last project. Then, in a couple of weeks, when he'd fully recovered, he would be on his way, back to his own life.

She heated up a cup of breakfast coffee and took it into the spare bedroom her father had used as a study, along with the records she had retrieved from the studio. The room looked out over the beach, so that she had a clear view of the shoreline, a pair of high-powered binoculars nearby for closer inspection of wildlife.

She spread her records out on top of the desk, sat down and began to read them over.

*   *   *

That afternoon, a south wind came up and a gentle rain began to fall, a sure harbinger of warmer weather. Sarah had worked steadily most of the day, taking time out only for a quick lunch and a short walk around the property to see if there was any more clearing away she had to do.

As she passed by the studio, there was no sign of Ross. The place looked totally uninhabited. Then, as she strolled up by the road, she noticed that his car was gone, and her heart gave a great leap. Surely he wouldn't have tried to drive! She almost ran back to the studio to find out if he was still there, but checked herself just in time. Most likely he'd asked Timothy to see about having his car towed away, or called the garage himself.

That evening, she fixed herself a quick supper of soup and a grilled cheese sandwich and sat at the kitchen table eating it and leafing through the notes she'd made that day. But somehow she couldn't concentrate. The house seemed so quiet, so empty. She kept glancing out the window, expecting . . .

Expecting what? Ross? She laughed aloud at her own foolishness. She was only afraid he'd make a pest of himself, expect to be waited on or entertained. If he really meant it when he said that he wouldn't get in her way, she should be grateful.

But when there was still no sign of him at all the next day, she began to grow seriously worried about him. She kept thinking about that last dizzy spell, Timothy's warnings about the possible aftermath of concussion. He could be lying there unconscious, with no way to call for help. Or dead!

She tried to work sporadically throughout the day, but couldn't seem to focus her mind on it. Finally, she threw her pencil down on top of the desk and put her head in her hands, groaning aloud. She'd just have to check on him, for her own peace of mind, out of common humanity.

The rain had stopped during the night, and the same south wind had brought with it a definite rise in temperature. There was a brisk breeze, but a mild one. With any luck, there would be a short spell of Indian summer before winter set in.

With only a thin sweater on over her cotton shirt, Sarah started down the path to the studio. At the door she hesitated for a moment, listening. Not a sound came from inside, and her heart started thudding heavily. She really should have checked on him sooner.

She raised a hand and knocked loudly on the door, then stood there waiting, shivering in the warm sunshine, hardly daring to breathe. Should she just walk in?

Then, at last, she heard footsteps on the other side, and she felt almost giddy with relief. He wasn't unconscious, wasn't dead! But when he opened the door, she could see that his face was still pale under the dark stubble, haggard even, and his eyes rather bleary, as though she'd just woken him.

"Yes?" he said.

"Uh," she stammered when she finally found her voice. She cleared her throat. "That is, I just thought I'd better check on you. I hadn't seen or heard any sign of you since yesterday morning," she hastened to explain. "And I was getting a little worried."

"That was very thoughtful of you," he said politely. "But I seem to be managing so far. Just a little tired."

"No troubling symptoms, then?" she asked brightly.

Her voice sounded brittle in her ears, too bright and she cursed the impulse that had brought her here.

"No, not really," he replied.

"What does that mean?" she asked, suddenly suspicious he was hiding something from her.

He shrugged. "Just that I still feel a little wobbly, and the ribs bother me if I sleep on them wrong. But I'm following Timothy's advice and just taking it easy. In fact, I've been reading through some of your father's old publications. I hope you don't mind."

"No, of course not. I hope you find them interesting."

"Very."

There was a short, awkward silence then. Sarah couldn't think of another thing to say, but neither could she come up with a graceful way to make her exit.

"Well," she said at last, "as long as you're all right, I guess I'll get back to work."

"How is it going?"

"Oh, fine," she said airily. "I'm making progress anyway."

"Good."

"Well, if you need anything, let me know."

He only nodded.

There was nothing for it after that but to give him a weak smile, turn around and go back to the house. Not a very warm reception, she thought as she trudged along. But he was still weak, probably in pain. And obviously wanted to be left alone.

She didn't see him at all for the next few days, but then one morning as she was working at her desk, actually making some headway, something caught her eye through the open window. Someone was running along the beach. A tall figure. A man. Ross!

She jumped to her feet. Was he crazy? Did he *want* a punctured lung? Did he have some kind of death wish? Then, slowly, she made herself sink back in her chair. He was a grown man. If he wanted to kill himself, let him.

She tried to get back to work, but after a futile half hour gave it up. The fine anger that had begun to simmer in her at the sight of him running was now reaching a slow boil. If he could exert himself like that, then it was time he left. And she'd go down to the studio right now and tell him so.

Quickly, before she could change her mind, she marched directly out to the studio and rapped smartly on the door, all primed to do battle. He answered it almost immediately, and when he did, all she could do was gaze up at him wide-eyed and openmouthed. The transformation in him was mind-boggling.

He had on a pair of dark trousers, well tailored to fit his long-legged, lean-hipped figure, and an obviously very expensive light blue knit shirt, open at the neck to reveal the long column of his throat.

Although his dark hair was a little too long, it looked as though he'd just washed it. It gleamed with reddish highlights in the sunshine and was still a little damp in spots. He had also shaved closely. Gone was the dark stubble that had shadowed his face since he'd first arrived. Instead, his tanned cheeks and square jaw were smooth, revealing clefts at either side of his mouth that deepened as he smiled down at her.

"Sarah!" he exclaimed.

The broad grin of obvious pleasure almost disarmed her, but then she remembered just in time why she had come, and she hardened her heart against him and his great smile and wonderful looks.

"I came to ask you when you planned to leave," she said.

He frowned, puzzled. "Leave? I'm not planning to go anywhere. What made you think that?"

She gave him a cold stare. "Well, when I saw you out running earlier, I naturally assumed you must be well enough to go."

"Oh, that," he said, his face clearing. "I just thought I'd try a little workout, just to get the stiffness out. But I didn't go far," he added hastily. "I'm still a lot weaker than I thought."

She eyed him suspiciously. Was he trying to pull a fast one on her? Faking it? Just how gullible did he think she was?

"A few days ago, you were at death's door," she commented dryly. "Today you're running."

"Listen," he went on, his voice low and persuasive, "I know how it must have looked. But ask yourself. Why would I try to deceive you into thinking I was worse off than I actually am?"

Then, in a flash, as though to prove his point, his eyes glazed over, his face blanched, and he started to sway.

Alarmed in spite of herself, Sarah's immediate instinct was to reach out and grab hold of him before he fell. But she stifled it in a hurry. Instead, she crossed her arms in front of her and watched him carefully. If it was an act, she had to admit it was a pretty good one. In fact, he almost had her convinced it was genuine, and she began to have second thoughts.

That is, until she saw him raise his eyes and give her a quick, piteous look. Then the corners of his mouth began to twitch. He straightened up and heaved a deep sigh.

"See?" he said accusingly. "I *am* still weak."

She continued to gaze at him in stony silence. Then, gradually, the twitch around his mouth broadened into a rather sheepish grin and a low chuckle rose from his throat.

He made such a comical picture that for the life of her she couldn't keep a straight face and soon found herself laughing along with him.

"That was quite a performance," she said at last. "Another few seconds and you might have had me convinced."

"Well, it wasn't entirely an act," he said. "Ask Timothy. He made the diagnosis after all. I didn't dream it up. And you were the one who insisted he examine me." He gave her another smile. "Now, why don't you come inside and have a cup of coffee with me? We can talk it over."

For a moment, she was definitely tempted, in fact just about to agree, but on closer inspection of the guileless look on his face, she decided she didn't quite like the gleam in his eye. It seemed almost predatory, and she was immediately on guard, all her defenses raised again.

"I don't think so," she said stiffly.

"Oh, come on, Sarah, lighten up." His mouth drooped. "It's lonely out here all by myself. I've started talking to the walls. Just a quick cup. You can tell me what you've been doing, how the work is coming along."

He put a hand on her arm, and at the touch, gentle but firm, little shivers began to run up and down her spine. Slowly, she withdrew her arm from his grasp.

"No," she said firmly. "Better not."

His face fell for a moment, but he recovered quickly and gave an offhand shrug of his broad shoulders. "All right. Have it your way. I'd just like to get to know you better, that's all." His eyes swept over her lazily. "What are you afraid of, Sarah?" he asked quietly. "I'd never harm you."

"Oh, I know that."

"Then what is it? The running? Do you still think I've been deceiving you?"

As a matter of fact she did, rather, but even those suspicions didn't seem very important at the moment. For some reason, she felt she had to get out of there, away from this man's disturbing presence. Now. Before it was too late.

"I'm not really sure," she hedged. "I just don't think it would be such a good idea."

He heaved an exasperated sigh. "All right, do as you like. But I can't see for the life of me what you're afraid of."

* * *

The weather continued clear and balmy. Ross had been staying in the studio for almost a week now, and after that last day there had been no further communication between them whatsoever. Except for the brief glimpses she caught of him from time to time out the window as he walked along the shore, he could have left for all she knew.

It was unnatural to be living so close to another human being yet never even pass the time of day with him. Of course, she reminded herself constantly, it had been her rule. She was the one who'd wanted to be left alone. Why should she complain when he kept his word and honored her own wishes?

Finally, after an entire morning spent at her desk making absolutely no headway, she knew she had to do something, take some action, or go stark raving mad. Then it came to her. She'd take a drive into the village. She needed to stock up on her dwindling supplies anyway, maybe buy herself a steak to barbecue outside this evening.

She jumped up from her chair, almost knocking it over in the process, and headed for the door, stopping only to retrieve her handbag from the kitchen counter where she'd left it last. Outside, she headed for the carport on the sheltered side of the house.

The car hadn't been used for weeks, and as always, she approached the temperamental beast with some trepidation. She knew there was plenty of gas because she'd just filled the tank the day before the big storm hit, but when she turned the key in the ignition and stepped on the gas, nothing happened.

She tried again. This time there was a low, whining sound, but the engine wouldn't catch. She kept on pumping the gas pedal, knowing in her heart it was probably the worst thing she could do, but so anxious by now to get out of there that she was past reason.

Finally, she gave up. It was hopeless. Tears of frustration smarted behind her eyes, and she banged her fists fruitlessly on the steering wheel, as though to beat the beast into submission. She couldn't walk the five miles to the village; she couldn't go back in the house and try one last time to get some work done. She'd just have to call the garage to come out and fix whatever was wrong.

Then suddenly, in the rearview mirror, she caught a brief glimpse of movement, a shadowy figure, and the next thing she knew, Ross was leaning down at her open window, his arms braced on the door frame, peering in at her.

"Need some help?" he asked.

"Obviously" was the tart reply. Then she sighed. "Sorry. It's not your fault. I'm just so frustrated...."

"Sounds as though you've flooded the engine," he said. He raised his head and sniffed the air, then grinned at her. "Smells like it, too. The place reeks of gasoline. Would you like me to try?"

"Please," she said, sliding over to the passenger seat.

Without another word, he got inside the car, turned the key, then immediately stomped down hard on the gas pedal, flooring it. The starter made the same whining, grinding noise as before, but he kept his foot firmly on the pedal, until finally the engine sputtered and slowly coughed into life.

"There," Ross said when it was purring nicely. "That should do it."

She laughed. "I could have done that myself."

"Sure you could," he replied. "The question is, why didn't you?"

"Right," she agreed, nodding. "You have a point. But what I know about cars you could put on the head of a pin. My father always took care of the beast. Anyway, thanks for bailing me out."

"Where are you off to?" he asked.

"The village. I need to do some grocery shopping."

"Mind if I tag along? I'd like to check on my car."

"Not at all," she said. "You can even drive. That is," she added hastily, "if you feel up to it."

"Oh, yes," he said. "I'll just take it slow and easy." Then he flashed her a grin. "And if I collapse at the wheel, you can take over."

He glanced briefly over the instruments, then released the hand brake, put the gear in reverse and started backing out of the carport, every motion assured, confident and relaxed.

Watching him, Sarah noticed that he had on a different shirt this morning, this one a pale yellow, and the same dark trousers. He looked as though he'd just stepped out of the shower, and once again she was impressed with how great he looked with a close shave and clean, well-brushed hair.

She shuddered to think what she must look like, without a trace of makeup on her face, still dressed in her shabby old denims and shapeless cotton shirt.

She'd been in such a hurry to get out of the house that she hadn't given a thought to her appearance. Then, with a shock, it came to her that she'd even combed her hair back carelessly that morning and tied it with a piece of string.

A piece of string! Somehow that was the crowning, humiliating blow. Could she somehow get rid of it while he was preoccupied with his driving?

Not a chance! She'd just have to live with it. He already knew she was no man's idea of a sex goddess anyway, so she might as well relax and enjoy his company while it lasted. Besides, he was talking to her now, glancing over at her.

"Your car seems to be running smoothly enough now," he remarked. "Your father must have taken good care of it."

"Oh, he did," she replied. Then she had to smile. "I think men must be born knowing all about cars."

He threw back his head and laughed. "Now that's a sexist remark if I ever heard one. I'm sure your feminist sisters wouldn't approve."

"Maybe not," she agreed. "But since there aren't many feminists around here, I guess I'm safe." She leaned back against her door and turned to face him, his fine profile outlined against the tunnel of huge trees they were passing through. "So tell me," she said. "How are you feeling?"

"Great. Better every day. No more dizzy spells, and the ribs seem to be healing nicely. I figure another week, then I'll be on my way." He turned to give her a brief smile. "And out of your hair."

She laughed. "You haven't been in my hair. I've hardly seen you at all, in fact."

He gave her another sideways flick of the eye. "Well, that was our agreement, wasn't it?"

"Yes," she replied hastily. "It was. And I appreciate the way you've honored it." A barefaced lie, she thought, but what else could she say?

They had reached the village by now. It was just a block long with only the barest minimum in the way of shops, just enough to serve the needs of the sparse population in the area. She showed him where the grocery store was located, and he parked directly in front of it.

"Ah," she said when they had stepped out onto the cracked pavement, "that's real curb service."

He bowed briefly. "My pleasure. Now, if you'll point me in the direction of the garage, I'll let you get on with your shopping."

"Right," she said. "Just walk to the end of the block and turn the corner. You can't miss it."

"I'll meet you back at the car, then, but don't rush on my account."

He turned to go, and she stood there for a few moments watching him walk away from her, his back straight, his broad shoulders held high, but with a relaxed, easy gait, as graceful as an athlete, and once again she was struck by what an attractive man he was.

A nice one, too, she decided as she turned into the grocery store. There hadn't been a trace of condescension in his manner when he'd started the car for her. And he'd be leaving soon. Why not stop all this pretense of trying to work, and enjoy his company in the short time remaining? And why not start tonight?

Inside the store, she went straight to the meat counter, where she picked out two thick filet steaks. Then to the produce section for fresh greens, tomatoes, cucumbers, scallions and two beautiful Idaho potatoes. She picked up a can of their best coffee, some sour cream and then, on an impulse, a wickedly expensive bottle of imported Chardonnay.

When she'd finished, she went back outside. Ross hadn't returned yet, but by the time she'd stowed her groceries in the back seat, she saw him coming down the street, walking toward her, and her heart gave a leap. Why had she tried so hard to keep him at a distance? Why hadn't she seized the opportunity to get to know this good-looking, interesting—and just plain *nice*—man while she had the chance, instead of hiding behind her work?

"Well?" she said when he reached the car. "What's the prognosis?" Then she saw that he was scowling. "What's wrong? Bad news?"

"I'm afraid so," he said disgustedly. "Apparently, they have to send to Seattle for parts. It seems foreign cars are not their specialty, and they aren't equipped to repair them."

"Then you won't be able to leave as soon as you've planned?"

"Oh, don't worry," he replied, his face set in a grim, determined expression. "I'll think of something. There's always a way to get what you want if you want it badly enough. Did you finish your shopping?" She nodded. "Well, then, let's be on our way, shall we?"

The return drive to the house was a silent one. Ross seemed wrapped in his own thoughts, schemes no doubt about how to make his escape, while

Sarah's head was filled with thoughts of how to approach him about dinner that night now that his mood had changed so drastically. He had been so relaxed and pleasant before they set out. Now he seemed to have retreated into a world of his own, shut her out completely. Maybe she'd better forget the whole thing.

However, when they arrived back at the house, and he'd parked the car in the carport, his mood seemed to have changed again. Before they'd even gotten out of the car, he turned to her with one of his old smiles.

"Well, thanks for the lift. And the company. To tell you the truth, I've missed human companionship more than I'd realized these past several days."

"Well, then," she said impulsively, "why not join me for dinner tonight? I picked up some steaks to cook outside on the grill and there's plenty for both of us."

"Now, there's an idea," he said, grinning broadly. "I'd be delighted."

"Say around seven?" she said.

He nodded. "Seven it is."

By six-thirty that evening, Sarah was putting the finishing touches on her dinner. The weather had warmed up considerably during the day, and she'd decided it would be nice to eat out on the patio one last time before winter. The coals were lit, the table set, a pitcher of martinis was cooling in the fridge, the salad made and the potatoes in the oven.

She'd spent what seemed like hours that afternoon agonizing over what to wear. She had very little in her meager wardrobe to choose from, and she wanted to look her best tonight, just to prove to him that she could, and to make up for that awful piece of string.

Then she remembered a dress she'd bought especially for a dinner dance Timothy had taken her to a few summers ago. She'd worn it just that once, then tucked it far back in her closet, knowing she'd never have any use for it again.

She pushed aside all the sensible cotton blouses and shirtwaist dresses she owned until she finally found the garment, still sheathed in the plastic covering it had come in. It would be perfect, she decided, holding it up to her and studying her reflection in the mirror. Anyway, Timothy had liked it, in fact had made his first halfway serious attempt at lovemaking that night. He'd had too much to drink, however, and backed off the moment she'd put up the first sign of resistance.

It had been ruinously expensive, a beautifully cut white cotton, which would set off the remains of her summer tan nicely. It was a very simple style and not too dressy for an evening at home. The bodice was close fitting, with a square low neckline that was cut straight across, just skimming the upper swell of her firm breasts, and held up by thin straps.

That evening at six o'clock, wearing the white dress, she stood in front of the mirror, brushing her golden, sun-streaked hair until it gleamed, then let it fall in its natural wave to her shoulders. For the next half hour, she experimented clumsily with makeup, scrubbing it off in dismay at the artificial results, and finally settled for merely a dash of light coral lip gloss.

After one last satisfied glance in the mirror, she slipped a pair of white sandals on her bare feet, then went out onto the patio to wait for him.

When he arrived promptly at seven, she was bending over the barbecue, checking on the coals, and didn't hear him come up behind her until he spoke.

"Would you like me to tend to the fire?" he asked.

She turned around. He was dressed in the same clothes he'd worn that morning, but looked freshly shaven. He was standing so close to her now that she could smell the faint tang of his after-shave, the lingering odor of a minty toothpaste.

There was also an unfamiliar look on the lean, tanned face, a strange gleam in the clear gray eyes. For some reason, she couldn't quite look away from him, could only stand there, her gaze held in his, until finally his eyes flicked away and traveled over her face, then slowly, deliberately, down the length of her body.

Then, just as slowly, he raised his eyes to hers again. "You look good enough to eat yourself," he said in a low voice.

He made no move to widen the distance between them, and she herself couldn't seem to budge. Suddenly, with no warning, he reached out a hand and ran it over her hair at the back of her head. She still couldn't move a muscle, even when the hand began to pull her closer.

The next thing she knew, his arms had come around her, his cheek was pressed against hers, his hands moving slowly, sensuously over her back. She was too stunned to move, even to think, her head in a whirl, a strange, unfamiliar warmth stealing through her body. It was as though this was what she'd been waiting for ever since he'd first appeared, waiting for, in fact, all her life.

She felt his mouth grazing lightly over her cheek, seeking her mouth, then settling there, his lips playing with hers, and she melted against him, blindly giving herself up to the sweetness of his kiss, the feel of his long, hard body pressed against hers, the gentle rasp of his freshly shaven cheek.

It wasn't until his kiss became firmer, more serious, the tip of his tongue pushing against her lips, that the first little alarm went off in her head. Then when she felt one hand slide around from her back to settle at the base of her throat and begin to inch its way slowly but inexorably downward, she finally came to her senses.

With a muffled cry, she pulled away from him and stood there, a hand at her throat, glaring at him.

"What do you think you're doing?" she cried. "How dare you attack me like that!"

CHAPTER FIVE

"ATTACK you!" he shouted.

The look on his face was one of such stunned amazement that if she hadn't been so angry, it would have been funny. All the color had drained out of it, his eyes were staring, his mouth open.

"That's what I said," she retorted angrily. She felt in total command of the situation now. "Just what did you think you were doing?"

"Well, what was I supposed to think?" he demanded. "You invite me for dinner, put on that sexy dress...." He shook his head in sheer frustration. "Women!" he growled. "If that doesn't beat all."

"No!" she exclaimed. "You're not going to put me on the defensive like that. I invited you to dinner out of simple kindness, just a friendly dinner before you left. What you chose to read into it is your problem, not mine."

He was eyeing her carefully now, his head cocked to one side, and there was even the hint of a smile playing about his lips. She would *not* let him stare her down, she promised herself, and returned his gaze unflinchingly. He was entirely in the wrong here.

"I see," he finally drawled in a slow, maddening voice. "And that's why you beat me off the minute I touched you."

In spite of her best intentions, she could feel her face go up in flame. "You took me by surprise, that's all," she finally said.

"Hah!" he exploded. "That's rich." He leaned closer to her, his face only inches away from hers now, his eyes narrowed into slits and boring into her. "I may not have all the answers when it comes to you mysterious creatures, but I do know a little about body language and I *certainly* know when a woman is resisting and when she's with me." He reared back, put his hands on his hips and glared at her. "And believe me, lady, you were with me just then, every step of the way."

That came a little too near the bone for comfort, and she took immediate refuge in wounded dignity. "That may be *your* expert opinion," she bit out. "But you're wrong."

He raised one dark eyebrow. "Oh, really?" he drawled. "Come on, Sarah. You're lying to yourself and you know it."

A sudden suspicion flashed into her mind. "What's more," she said, pointing an accusing finger at him, "I have a sneaking hunch you've probably been shamming your injuries all along, making them seem worse than they really were just to play on my sympathy."

To her intense satisfaction, a deep red flush washed over *his* face now. Scowling darkly, he lowered his eyes and looked away. Aha! she thought. I've struck a nerve. But if so, he recovered quickly. He only shrugged and gave her a smug look.

"Ask Timothy, then," he said. "He's the one who kept insisting I take it easy. I think you're just blowing smoke."

Although the reminder of Timothy's insistence that he needed rest took the wind out of her sails somewhat, she was still convinced he'd used her, manipulated her, just to get her into bed, probably only because he was bored. All she wanted at this point was to get him out of the house, out of her life, before she made an even worse fool of herself than she already had.

"Think what you like," she said stiffly. "Right now I just want you to leave. You can stay the night, but tomorrow morning I want you out of here for good."

He gave her a crooked smile. "What about our agreement?"

"There is no agreement," she snapped. "You canceled that yourself when you deceived me, lied to me. I can't trust you."

His face grew pinched, drained of color, and she had a sudden insight into his true character. Beneath the brash exterior, he obviously thought of himself as an honorable man, and her accusation that he'd behaved less than honorably really stung.

"All right," he said quietly. "If that's how you feel, I'll leave first thing in the morning."

"Good!"

"But before I go," he went on, "I have just one last thing to say." He eyed her carefully for a moment, then went on in a low voice. "I made a move on you tonight honestly believing it was what you wanted, too, were even inviting." She opened her mouth to protest, but he held up a hand and kept on speaking in the same low monotone. "And you *did* respond. Don't even try to deny it. What's more, even if you're right that I've been pretending to be more badly hurt than I really was, doesn't it occur to you that I've gone to an awful lot of trouble over you?" He paused dramatically. "What I can't understand is why you feel so insulted just because I find you attractive, *worth* taking all that trouble over."

With that, he turned on his heel and walked slowly away from her, his hands in the pockets of his trousers, his gait unhurried and as self-assured as ever.

For a long time, she simply stood there staring after him, still stunned by his parting shot. Then, when he disappeared around the side of the house, she realized her mouth was still hanging open. She snapped it shut and sat down at the table. All the anger had drained out of her by this time, and she was already beginning to regret her hasty accusation.

Then slowly, mechanically, she began clearing off the table she'd set so carefully, putting away the food she'd prepared, moving in a trance like an automaton.

When she'd finished, she trudged wearily back to her bedroom and stood before the mirror staring at her reflection, her mind in a turmoil. The dress *was* rather seductive. She *had* gone to great pains to look attractive to him and she *was* the one who had invited him for dinner.

Besides that, now that her anger had drained away, she had to admit that she had grown fond of him. She had enjoyed his company today on their drive into the village. She did find him physically attractive, his personality compelling. She remembered, too, the interest he had taken in her as a person, how he had encouraged her to finish her education and go on with her father's work on her own.

And to be honest, she also had to admit that he was right about her response to his kiss. Much as she tried to deny it, she definitely had enjoyed the feel of those strong arms around her, the softened mouth pressed against hers, the long, hard body so close and so different from her own.

And even if he had deceived her a little about his injuries, what did that prove except that he found her desirable enough to take the trouble? Tears of regret began to smart behind her eyes and fall slowly, unchecked, down her cheeks. For the first time, it came to her just how lonely she'd really been since her father died.

She undressed slowly, then fell into bed with a troubled mind, half-convinced that she was the one who'd been in the wrong tonight, but without a clue as to what she could do about it now.

After a fitful sleep, Sarah awoke the next morning even more convinced that she'd done him an injustice last night. If so, it was up to her to swallow her pride and admit it. Besides that, she didn't want him to go. Was it too late? He could be gone already.

She jumped out of bed and dressed hurriedly in her old denims. No more seductive dresses for her! If he did stay, of course there could be no question of any lovemaking. She'd be in so far over her head with a man like Ross Kirk that she'd never survive it.

She splashed water on her face, brushed her teeth, then ran a comb through her hair and pulled it back, securing it with a clip this time, then ran to the door and stepped outside.

There was no sign of life at the studio. Had he left before she got up? She glanced at her watch. It was only eight o'clock. Surely he couldn't have left so early. How would he leave? She hadn't heard a taxi, and he wouldn't have walked to the village lugging his suitcase.

She hurried down the path, but as she approached the door, her steps slowed. What could she say? It wasn't going to be easy. How much humble pie would she have to eat and still maintain some semblance of dignity? Maybe she'd been too hasty. She really should take some time to think it over.

She had just made up her mind to turn back when the door opened, and Ross appeared. He just stood there gazing silently at her, his dark eyebrows raised in an inquiring look, as though waiting for her to speak.

"Uh, Ross," she finally stammered. "Could I talk to you for a minute?"

Immediately, he stood aside and made a wide gesture with one hand, waving her in. "Be my guest," he said in a toneless voice.

When she stepped inside, the first thing she noticed was his open suitcase on the bed, the pile of clothing and personal effects beside it. She stared dully at it for a moment, then sucked in a deep breath and turned to him.

"After thinking it over," she blurted out in a rush, "I've decided that you can stay on. That is, if you want to."

"Oh? What brought that on?"

"Well, we did have an agreement," she said in a clipped, no-nonsense tone.

"My, my," he commented dryly, going over to the bed to resume his packing. "Such graciousness overwhelms me. How could I resist?"

"Well, all right, then, go. It's up to you. I certainly don't care one way or the other. But I did tell you that you could stay until you were completely well, until your car was fixed anyway, and I don't like to break my word."

His hands stilled then. For several moments, he just stood there staring at the shirt he was holding, as though deep in thought. Then he set it down on the bed and turned to her.

"No," he said quietly, "you wouldn't. All right, I'll stay, at least until I can figure a way to get out of here."

She didn't like the way he made it sound, as though he was doing her a favor, but didn't want to argue about it. She'd done what she came to do. Now it was time to make a graceful exit.

"Well, that's settled. We'll just go on as we were before..." Her voice faltered, then she raised her chin and gave him a direct look. "Before last night," she added.

"Oh, you don't have to worry about that," he said with feeling. Then he smiled. "Once burned, twice shy, you know."

"Just so there's no misunderstanding," she said curtly. She turned around and marched out the door, her head held high.

There, she said to herself on her way back to the house. She'd handled that rather well, made it clear that he could stay, but only on her terms. But by the time she reached the house, her spirits had sagged. What had she really gained? And hadn't he been awfully too quick to agree to those terms?

It rained steadily for the next few days, just a light drizzle, but enough to keep Sarah indoors. Actually, this suited her quite well anyway. A school of porpoises had been sighted at a wildlife station farther south down the coast, and it was crucial that she get her records up-to-date before they reached her area.

She also wanted to avoid a meeting with Ross. There had been no sign of him, and not a sound to be heard from the studio. There was a telephone out there, so she assumed he could take care of any business with his car himself.

She had several wistful moments of wishing they could be friends again. She missed his company badly. Even in his most irascible moments, he had been amusing, stimulating, interesting, like a breath of fresh air in her drab life. But she knew in her heart they couldn't go back to that easy companionship. With that one kiss, they had stepped over a boundary in their relationship. It would never be the same again.

Although it took constant effort, she did manage to keep her mind firmly on her work, away from thoughts of him and their last sticky encounter.

He'd be gone soon. It was time she got on with her own life, such as it was. Even though it seemed rather dull and uninteresting now, still, it was her life and she had enjoyed it before he burst upon the scene.

By the end of the third day, the rain had stopped, the sun had come out from behind the thinning remnants of cloud cover, and Sarah was sick to death of her own company. Also, now that her records were finally complete, she was filled with such a feeling of accomplishment that she decided she'd give herself a reward.

She put her work away neatly and went to the telephone to call Carol. But when she lifted the receiver, she heard a man's voice. It must be Ross on the extension in the studio. She was just about to quietly replace the receiver when she heard a woman's light tinkling trill of laughter, then her voice.

"But, darling," Sarah heard her say, "we expected you back ages ago!"

"Well, I'm sorry, Sylvia, but I couldn't help it if a tree fell on my car, could I? Look at it from my point of view. I'm stuck here at the back of beyond with nothing to do but stare at the ocean and nurse my broken ribs while you're enjoying nightlife in the city. Don't worry, as soon as my car is repaired, I'll be out of here like a shot."

Her cheeks burning, Sarah carefully, quietly, replaced the receiver. Sylvia! She sounded so self-assured, so sophisticated, was probably gorgeous. And they had spoken in such intimate tones.

She waited a good five minutes, just staring down at the telephone as though it were alive and about to jump at her, until she dared to lift it up again. This time, there was only a familiar hum, and she dialed Carol's number.

"Hi, Carol," she said when her friend answered. "It's me, Sarah. How would you like to drive down to Ocean Shores with me this evening for dinner at that great new restaurant? My treat."

"Oh, honey, I'm sorry, I can't today. My daughter and her two children are up here visiting me from Portland for a few days, and I see them so seldom I just can't leave them."

"Of course," Sarah replied quickly. "I understand. That's great. I've been working so hard I just felt like giving myself a little treat. We can do it another time."

"Well, thanks for asking me anyway." Carol paused for a moment, then went on in an elaborately offhand voice. "By the way, how are you getting along with your star boarder by now? I notice he's still there."

"Oh, he's much better" was the hasty reply. Leave it to Carol, she groaned inwardly, to know every detail of everyone's business for miles around. "He's just staying on—in Dad's studio," she added pointedly, "until his car is repaired. Then he'll be leaving."

"Too bad," Carol said with a low, meaningful chuckle. "I saw him out swimming in the surf early yesterday morning, and I must say he's quite a fine figure of a man. He could be a film star, with all that black hair and those rippling muscles."

A sudden unbidden vision rose up in Sarah's mind of Ross rising from the waves, walking toward her, his arms outstretched, dressed only in a pair of swimming trunks....

"Sarah?" came Carol's sharp voice. "Are you still there?"

"Yes. Of course. My mind just wandered off for a minute."

"I see. Well, don't tell me you haven't noticed what a great-looking man he is." She sighed heavily. "Ah, if I were only twenty years younger! I'd jump at the chance of a man like that." She paused for a moment, but when Sarah didn't reply, went on kindly but firmly. "And I think you'd be a fool to pass it by."

"Oh, come on, Carol. You know nothing about him. Neither do I, for that matter." She gave a nervous laugh. "Except that I'm quite sure he's a man pretty well used to getting his own way with women, and I have no intention of leaving myself open for that kind of trouble."

"So you might get hurt. Are you any better off burying yourself down here with your whales and porpoises? You're what, twenty-five years old? A lovely young girl like you," she chided, "and you haven't even lived yet. Besides," she added with another low chuckle, "even if he is the love 'em and leave 'em type, what a memory you'd have!"

"Well, thanks for the advice," Sarah replied dryly. "But even if I wanted to follow it, he'll be out of here soon, and I won't get the chance. Anyway," she rushed on to avoid any more discussion, "I hope you enjoy your family's visit."

They hung up then, and Sarah sat there staring
dully at the telephone for several moments, unable
to shake off the impact of her friend's comments.
Could she possibly be right?

No, she decided, jumping up from the chair. So
she was twenty-five and had no experience with
men. She had her work, didn't she? Her home, her
friends. It was a good life. And when he was gone,
the painful ache in her heart and loins would go
with him.

Late that afternoon, she took a long walk up the
beach, just to get the kinks out from sitting at that
desk for so long. By the time she headed back
toward home, the sun was beginning to set beneath
the western horizon, casting a wide swath of gold
and red over the gentle swell of the sea. The tide
was coming in, lapping gently against the sandy
shore, and the screeching gulls swooped low, scav-
enging for their last meal of the day.

As she came around the last wide bend, she could
just see her house, and was filled with a sudden
warm glow at the familiar sight. She felt much
better after the long walk and had even managed
to put the conversation with Carol out of her mind.
It was very peaceful in the balmy evening air, a
slight breeze warm on her face and arms.

Then, as she neared the house, she noticed that
someone was standing on the shoreline, looking out
over the darkening blue of the sea. It had to be
Ross, and she stopped in her tracks, staring.

His back was toward her, and he was dressed only
in a pair of low-slung jeans, his hands stuck in the
back pockets. His upper body was bare, the tape

still binding his ribs. As she wondered what he was looking at so intently, her eyes traveled along his line of vision, out over the ocean.

At that moment, two sleek gray porpoises leaped together out of the water, a good three feet into the air, then dived back, just as though they were playing a game. Sarah watched entranced as their snouts broke the water again, thinking she must make a note of their appearance. She glanced at her watch to check the time, and when she looked up again, she saw that Ross had turned and was now gazing fixedly at her.

Their eyes met and held, and a silent, unspoken communication seemed to pass between them, almost like a charge of electricity. He began to walk slowly toward her, and she found herself moving in his direction, almost against her will.

When they finally met, they stood there wordlessly, inches away from each other, eyes still locked together. Sarah's pulse was pounding erratically, she had trouble breathing, and a heated glow was spreading through her body. Still, she couldn't make herself look away from those mesmerizing deep gray eyes.

Suddenly, she felt herself swaying toward him, heard a low, sighing groan escape her throat, and in the next moment was in his arms, clinging to him, all her good intentions and sensible warnings simply flying out the window. All she knew was that this was where she wanted to be. The consequences simply didn't matter anymore.

"Sarah," she heard him murmur in her ear as he pulled her more tightly to him. "Sarah. You'll never know how badly I've wanted to hold you like this again."

There was no mistaking the genuine ache in his voice, and for the first time she grasped the fact that she also wielded power over him. She ran her hands up into his thick dark hair and smiled up into his eyes. What she saw there filled her with love. He *wants* me, her heart sang. He *desires* me. And I want him. Nothing else seemed to matter.

He kissed her then, a long, slow exploration of her mouth that left her weak and longing for more. Then, suddenly, his lips left hers. He raised his head, put his hands on her shoulders and moved slightly back from her, breaking their body contact.

Alarmed at his abrupt withdrawal and still reeling from the impact of his kiss, Sarah stared up at him. The sky was rapidly growing dark now that the sun had set, and his face was cast in shadows. Still, she could make out the expression on his face as he gazed down deeply into her eyes without speaking, his expression so grave it was almost a frown, and her heart gave a great lurch. Something was wrong.

"Ross, what is it?"

Then he smiled. "Sarah," he said softly, running a hand over her face and smoothing her hair back from her forehead. "Lovely Sarah. Are you sure you want this? Do you know where it's leading?"

"What—what do you mean?" she stammered.

As though sensing her hurt and confusion, he gathered her to him again, tucked her head under his chin and began speaking again in a low, serious voice. "You know by now how much I want you, don't you?" She could only nod. "And I think," he went on carefully, "that you want me, too."

She hesitated for a moment, then raised her head to look up at him. "Yes," she said, "I do." Then she frowned. "Just what is it you're trying to say, Ross?"

He gave her a crooked smile. "I guess I'm not quite sure. For the first time in living memory, I'm at a loss for words—the right words—in a situation like this."

"Well, then," she said, nestling closer to him and putting her arms around his waist, "why say anything at all?"

"Because I don't want to harm you in any way. I like you, Sarah. I care for you a lot. And I also respect you. When I needed help, you took me in knowing nothing about me. You nursed me, put up with my bad temper, fed me, gave me a place to stay. I don't want to take advantage of you, or hurt you, in any way. I know how inexperienced you are—"

"That's my lookout, isn't it?" she broke in firmly. "It seems to me now that I was only half-alive before you came. I'm a grown woman, not a child who needs to be protected from the harsh realities of life. I told you I wanted you. You say you want me. Isn't that enough?"

He shook his head. "Not always," he replied in a voice tinged with melancholy. "Wanting doesn't have to lead to doing, may even be a terrible mistake, especially when there are risks involved. I'm a rolling stone, Sarah. I can't offer you anything permanent or lasting. And I have ties to the past that I still need to resolve."

Sarah's heart turned to stone within her. "Are you trying to tell me you're married?"

"No, of course not. I wouldn't do a thing like that. In fact, my respect for the institution is one of the reasons I'm not married, probably never will be. Not the way things are today."

"Then why are you telling me all this?" she asked impatiently.

"I just don't want there to be any misunderstandings."

She raised her hands to his face, her fingers tracing the bony ridge of his jawline, the deep clefts at the sides of his mouth, the high cheekbones, and smiled at him.

"Fair enough," she said. "I'll consider myself warned. Now, are you going to kiss me again or not?"

"Oh, Sarah," he breathed, clasping her tightly to him. "What a miracle you are!"

As though a spring had been released within him, all restraint vanished. His mouth opened wide, pressing against hers and pulling at her lips so hard that her flesh felt bruised. His probing tongue thrust past her teeth to fill the inside of her mouth, and she felt as though she were drowning in his fiery embrace.

One hand moved to the base of her throat, lingered there for a moment, then slowly slid downward to cover her breast. Sarah drew in a sharp breath at the sweetness of his touch, the fire it aroused deep within her, and she pressed her lower body more tightly against his, his hard need unmistakable against her thigh.

They sank down together on the cool sand, the waves lapping against the shore the only sound to be heard in the stillness of the evening. The moon had risen high in the sky by now, a brilliant harvest moon that was just bright enough for her to see the rapt expression on his face, the gleam in the glazed gray eyes.

Leaning over her, he slowly unbuttoned her shirt and spread it open. He gazed down at her bare breasts for a long moment, then began to stroke them. With a low moan of pleasure, Sarah closed her eyes and gave herself up totally to the sheer joy of the present moment.

He was a thoughtful and generous lover, as concerned for her satisfaction as his own, and when they were both naked, he hovered over her, waiting for her to show him where she wanted him to go, until finally, with a great gasp of release, he carried her over the top with him until they were both falling, falling, on the other side of paradise.

From then on, every day became filled with delight for Sarah. And, she believed, for Ross, too. Regardless of appearances, he moved into the house, into her bedroom, that very night.

They took long walks together, hand in hand, up and down the beach, exploring the tide pools and rocky caverns like children, and long nights of ever-increasing intimacy in their lovemaking. And they talked. At last he opened up to her unreservedly about his life, his hopes, his fears, his desires, and she learned to her amazement that in many ways he was as confused about his future as she was herself.

"I grew to hate the family business," he told her late one evening when they were sitting side by side in the living room with a roaring fire, his arm around her, her head on his shoulder. The weather had turned cold again, and they enjoyed the cozy nights of solitude, as though the world outside didn't exist. "Not only the business," he went on, "but the life I was living. It's the real reason I left, came on this trip by myself, to sort things out in my own mind."

"And have you?" she asked quietly.

"Not entirely." He didn't speak for several moments, and somehow she knew instinctively that there was more, that he needed to tell her something but wasn't quite sure how to do it. "To be honest with you," he finally admitted, "there was a woman involved."

Sylvia! she thought in a sudden panic. Although she believed she had accepted the fact that her affair with Ross wasn't permanent, that she'd never be able to keep him, she couldn't bear the thought of another woman possessing what she couldn't have herself. She remained silent, hoping he would go on, steeling herself for the worst.

"It was another family thing," he said at last. "She's the daughter of my father's business partner. Both families were pushing hard for an engagement. She's a nice enough girl. We sort of grew up together. But I didn't love her, and I especially didn't want one more tie to the business."

"What about her?" she asked. "Does she love you?"

"I doubt it. I think she wanted a suitable husband more than anything else." He drew her closer and tilted her head up so that he could look down into her eyes. "It took knowing you, caring for you, knowing you cared for me, to teach me what love between a man and a woman could be.''

Sarah's heart soared. Could he be saying what she thought, what she hoped, he might be saying? All of a sudden, it came to her that it was time for her to take the greatest risk of her life, make herself totally vulnerable to this man, simply by telling him the truth that was in her heart.

She took a deep breath, then looked directly into his eyes. ''I do love you, Ross,'' she said quietly.

For a moment, he seemed utterly taken aback, even startled. Then, gradually, he relaxed, his features softened, and he put a hand on her face. ''Yes,'' he said, ''I know you do.'' Then he gave her a wry smile. ''And in spite of all my best intentions, I'm afraid I've fallen into the same trap I warned you against. I've fallen in love with you, too, helplessly, hopelessly.'' He frowned as though deep in thought for a moment, and Sarah held her breath, waiting, until he spoke again. ''Now,'' he went on in a brisker tone, ''the question is what to do about it.''

If he'd told her to jump into the ocean, Sarah would have done it in a shot. At that moment, basking in the knowledge of his love, she would have done anything he asked of her.

''First of all,'' he said in the same businesslike tone, ''now that my car is ready, I've got to go back.'' As though sensing her hurt, he hastened to reassure her. ''Sarah, I must. I can't plan a future with you until I settle a few issues from the past, make it clear to my family, to that whole world, that I can't go along with what they want anymore. You do understand, don't you, darling?''

Although icy fingers had twined around her heart at the thought of losing him, even for a short time, she knew he was right. "Yes," she said at last, "I do understand."

"As soon as I get things squared away at home, I'll come back, I promise. And in the meantime, I'll call you, keep you posted how things are going. All right?"

She nodded and forced out a smile. "All right," she agreed. "When will you leave?"

He gave her a knowing grin and leaned over to kiss her eyes, her cheeks, his lips coming to rest on her mouth. "Not tonight," he murmured against her lips as his hand moved to her breast. "That's for sure."

That night, his lovemaking was even more passionate, more intense than ever before. It was as though he wanted to make himself a part of her, to leave something of himself within her, before he left.

But in the morning, after he'd shaved, he hadn't changed his mind. While he packed his things, she fixed him a big breakfast, and later, as they sat across from each other at the kitchen table eating, she couldn't keep her eyes off him. She wanted to memorize every plane and feature of his face, every angle and muscle of his long, hard body.

After breakfast, they said their final goodbyes, and he kissed her for the last time, a long, sweet kiss that made it even harder to lose him. Now that he'd made his decision, he seemed anxious to be on his way. All she could do was let him go.

But as she stood in front of the house and watched him drive away, staring after him until his car rounded the last bend and disappeared from view, the tears fell unchecked down her face. She had never felt so bereft in her life.

CHAPTER SIX

THE rest of that day was the longest Sarah had ever spent. She kept wandering distractedly from room to room looking for traces of him, anything to keep the memory of those golden days alive.

But he'd only been with her for such a short time that he'd left no sign he'd ever stayed there at all. There were only the dishes he'd eaten out of at breakfast that morning, and even those he had rinsed and left to soak in the kitchen sink.

There had to be *something* of his left behind in the studio, some tangible reminder of his presence, but she couldn't quite make herself go down there to find out.

She took a long walk down the beach that afternoon, going deliberately in the opposite direction from Carol's. She was in no mood for casual conversation or her friend's probing questions. For now, all she wanted was to dwell on the joys of the time she'd spent with Ross, the love she felt for him swelling in her breast until it felt as though it would burst.

When the telephone rang that evening, she was in the kitchen, searching listlessly through the cupboards for something that might tempt her appetite. She ran to the counter and snatched up the receiver on the second ring.

"Oh, Ross," she breathed when she heard his voice. "I'm so glad you called. Where are you?"

"Some dinky little town in Oregon near the California border. It looks as though I'll have to spend the night here instead of driving straight through as I'd planned."

"I see. You're probably tired and still not quite feeling up to par from your accident."

"No. I feel fine. It's just that the highway patrol has issued a storm warning for the Siskiyou Mountains, and tire chains are advised," he explained. "And since I don't have any with me, I decided it was better not to try to drive over the pass at night. I'll wait and see what it looks like in the morning."

"Please be careful. Those mountain roads can be treacherous if it snows and they ice over."

"Well, we'll hope it won't snow. I'm really anxious to get going." He paused for a moment, then went on in a lower, more intimate voice. "Are you missing me as much as I miss you?"

Her heart soared. "Not really," she said in an offhand tone. Then laughed. "Of course I am. More, I'm sure. At least you have something to take your mind off . . . well, other things."

"No" was the firm reply. "I don't. I keep thinking about those other things until I'm ready to turn around and come back."

"So, why don't you?"

"I can't," he said with a sigh of genuine regret. "Not until I settle things at home. But it won't be long. I know now what I've got to do. And you're a major part of my future plans. You know that, don't you?"

"Yes, Ross," she said, "I know that. And I'll be here, waiting for you."

"Well, I'd better go see if I can find a place to eat, then look for a motel. If I've got to drive over the mountains tomorrow in a blizzard, I'll need a good night's sleep. I'll call you as soon as I get to San Francisco, tomorrow sometime, hopefully."

"I'll be here," she said again.

When they'd hung up, Sarah sat on the stool at the kitchen counter, her chin resting in her hand, smiling dreamily into space, basking in the glow of that conversation. Just hearing the sound of his voice again had raised her spirits immeasurably.

All of a sudden, she felt ravenous, filled with energy and purpose. She went to the fridge and took out the remains of the ham they'd had for dinner the night before and a bowl of potato salad, then dished them up and sat down at the table to eat, her mind and heart still filled with thoughts of the tall dark man she had come to love beyond life itself.

The next morning, however, her euphoria had fled, and the days that followed were the bleakest Sarah had ever known. Not even the aftermath of her father's death had hit her so hard.

It was as though, after she'd tasted paradise, spent those few short weeks in such perfect bliss, everything else seemed empty, meaningless. She knew that much of the unremitting gloom came from her anxiety about the future, but still couldn't quite shake it.

There was no doubt in her mind that Ross loved her, and she kept reminding herself of the joy he had brought into her life, his solemn promise to return. But how would it all end? He had never breathed a word about marriage, and there was still his engagement, unofficial as it might be, probably to the lovely Sylvia.

Of course, she would have to be lovely. That voice she'd heard on the telephone still haunted her. It had sounded so self-assured, so confident that Ross already belonged to her. He'd said he was going to take care of it. But then what?

The next day, she moved her records back into the studio. It was more convenient since all her father's files and journals were kept there, but mainly she felt closer to Ross in the place where he had stayed, as though a faint, lingering aura of his presence still remained, even though he wasn't there in the flesh.

She kept coming across little reminders of him. A bar of his soap still in the dish in the shower stall, its fresh scent achingly familiar to her. A used razor blade set carefully on the glass shelf over the bathroom sink, a few tiny bristles from his beard still clinging to the surface. The sheets of the bed he had slept in, still faintly redolent of his distinctive, clean fragrance. A scattering of dark hairs on the pillowcase where his head had lain.

Their nightly telephone conversation was the high point of each day. He had called her, as promised, the very next night from his condo in San Francisco to let her know he had made it safely over the mountains.

"I didn't know you lived in a condo," she said, laughing. "In fact, I don't really know anything about how you live, what your daily life is really like."

"Well," he replied, "there really isn't that much to tell."

"Yes, but if I had more details, then I'd feel you were closer. I could picture you doing certain things, even little unimportant things. You've seen me in my home after all. I have no image at all of yours."

"It's not going to be my home much longer," he said firmly. "Remember, the only reason I even came back here was to cut loose from it. It won't be long. Try to be patient. It's as hard for me as it is for you."

Sarah doubted that. Men seemed to have a way of losing themselves in other things, while most women filled their whole lives with love. What was it Lord Byron had said? "Man's love is of man's life a thing apart; 'Tis womans' whole existence."

That wasn't quite as true today as it used to be. Women did have work of their own to interest them. They didn't need to make men their "whole existence." Still, it did seem to work out that way in spite of their new freedom from traditional roles.

"I know," she said at last. "I don't mean to complain. I just miss you, that's all. I can't really *see* you in the place where you are. It's as though you only exist here, at the beach."

"I know, darling. I feel much the same way. But you must understand, I can't just pick up and leave. It wouldn't be fair to my family, my friends, the business. Or to you. I want us to start out with a clean slate. Don't you see?"

"Oh, yes," she assured him. "And you must take all the time you need. I don't mean to rush you. So long as I know you still care, still want me."

"Of course I do. You must believe that."

* * *

The next night, the telephone rang just around the time Ross usually called, but when she answered it, Carol's voice came on the line.

"Well," she said, heaving a heartfelt sigh of relief, "the family finally left. I love my grandchildren, but I'll have to admit they can get wearing after a few weeks of trying to keep up with them. Where do they get all that energy?"

Sarah laughed. "Oh, I suppose we had it once, too."

"If so, I don't remember" was the dry response. "Anyway," she went on briskly, "I just called to take you up on your dinner invitation. Would tonight be good? I could use a break."

"Well," Sarah hedged, "I can't leave just yet. I'm expecting a telephone call."

"Oh?" Then Carol chuckled deep in her throat. "Could it be from the hunk? I noticed he was gone."

Sarah fought down a sudden surge of irritation. "Carol, is there anything you don't notice?" she asked lightly.

"Well, excuse me!" Carol replied huffily. "I certainly don't mean to pry. Seems to me you're a mite touchy about that man."

"Oh, I'm sorry, Carol. I didn't mean to snap at you. And I'd like to go out to dinner tonight. Just give me half an hour or so, and I'll drive to your place and pick you up. All right?"

The glitzy new restaurant in Ocean Shores, a booming summer resort some twenty miles south of the village, was clearly designed as a tourist attraction. Heavy rope seine nets were draped on the walls, these were several round, pale green glass Japanese fishing floats scattered about, glittering in the subdued lighting, a few crab pots and lots of driftwood, and against one wall a huge saltwater aquarium was filled with smaller sea creatures and aquatic plants.

It was also very noisy, and the prices ruinously expensive. When the two women were seated at a minute table and handed menus by a subservient young waiter oozing false heartiness and charm, it was all Sarah could do to keep from gasping aloud.

After one glance, Carol leaned across the table and spoke in a hushed voice. "I think we'd better go Dutch."

"No," Sarah insisted, "it's my treat."

She quailed inwardly at what this would do to her budget, but felt she owed it to her friend for the way she'd been neglecting her lately, not to mention her sharp tone earlier.

"Anyway," Carol said, "let me buy the wine. Or would you prefer a cocktail?"

"No. Wine sounds great." She glanced over the menu again. "Let's splurge and have lobster. How about it?"

"Well, if you're sure you can afford it."

"Yes. Absolutely."

The waiter returned just then and Carol ordered a bottle of Riesling. When it was served, she held up her glass in a toast.

"Here's to you, kiddo," she said, gazing at Sarah across the table, a sharp gimlet gleam in her eyes. "And I must say, you're looking great. That dusty green color just suits you, and I like the way you're letting your hair hang loose."

"Why, thank you, Carol," Sarah replied, pleased.

"There's a real bloom on you, too," Carol went on. "In fact, you look just like..." She hesitated a moment, then plunged ahead, a defiant note in her voice. "Just like a woman in love."

Sarah immediately felt her face go up in flame. She lowered her eyes and took a quick sip of wine to cover her confusion, knowing in her heart it was a forlorn hope. Nothing escaped Carol. But why try to hide it? Actually, she would welcome a chance to talk about it. Somehow that might make it all seem more real.

"I'm sorry," Carol was saying stiffly. "As usual, I can't keep my mouth shut." Then her voice softened. "But I do care, Sarah, and I want you to be happy."

"I know," Sarah replied. She reached across the table to touch her friend lightly on the arm. "And you're right, of course." She smiled. "I just didn't realize it showed that much."

"Do you want to talk about it? Or should I keep quiet?"

"Oh, there really isn't that much to tell. I mean, yes, you're right. I guess I do love him. I *know* I do. But I really don't know where it's all leading."

"Have you heard from him since he left?"

"Oh, yes. He calls me every night."

"Well, then. I'd say that's certainly an indication it's leading somewhere. What do you know about him?"

Sarah told her the bare facts of Ross's life, ending with his determination to break free from a world that had no more meaning for him. "That's really why he went back. He feels there are a lot of loose ends he needs to tie up in San Francisco, both business and personal, before he can move on to what he really wants.''

''I see. And what's that?''

Sarah gave her a blank look. ''What's what?''

''What is it he really wants?''

''Well, I'm not sure of the details,'' Sarah replied slowly. ''We never really got into that. I do know that his family is involved in several enterprises, so I guess I just assumed that Ross would continue working for them, only in a different way.''

''And then what?'' Carol asked. ''I mean, after he gets these personal and business matters cleared up, where do you fit in?''

Since Sarah had no firm answer to that, in fact had been worrying about that very thing herself, she could only laugh dismissively. ''I'm afraid we haven't gotten that far quite yet.''

''I see.''

''Say, what is this, Carol?'' she asked playfully. ''Weren't you the one who was promoting a romance the minute you found out he was staying with me?'' She laughed. ''Not to mention that view you had of him swimming in the surf. As I recall, you were pretty impressed.''

Carol smiled. ''Yes, I was. And I wouldn't try to talk you out of a little fling for the world.'' Then she sobered. ''But if you'll recall, I also told you at the same time that there was a chance you could get hurt.''

Sarah lifted her chin. ''I know that, and I'm willing to risk it. But don't forget, you also said that the experience would be worth it. And,'' she added with a sly grin, ''you were right.''

Carol's eyes opened wide, and her mouth fell open. ''Well,'' she said at last, ''I must say the worm has really turned. You don't sound in the least like the old Sarah Wainwright.''

''That's because I'm not,'' Sarah replied firmly. ''Now, I see our waiter heading this way. Have we decided on the lobster?''

Two nights later, on a Thursday, Sarah sat glumly at the kitchen table, picking halfheartedly at her meal of warmed-up spaghetti, her eyes never straying far from the telephone on the counter, which remained absolutely, maddeningly, silent. It was quarter of seven, and no word yet from Ross.

Although she had told Carol the other evening that he called her every night, and that she wanted to wait for him before going out to dinner, the truth was he hadn't called that night, the first time he'd missed.

At first, she told herself he'd probably called later, while she was at dinner, cursed Carol for talking her into going out, and herself for giving in. But when there was no word from him the next night, or the one after that, she began to grow seriously alarmed. Maybe he'd had a relapse, or another accident, was lying unconscious in a hospital bed, unable to let her know. His family had probably never heard of her. Would he have mentioned her to them?

It dawned on her then that in spite of his promises, his obvious affection and unmistakable desire for her, his plans for their future, however unspoken, she actually existed totally on the fringes of his life. What did he do every day back in his old home, his familiar surroundings? Who did he talk to? What was his work like? Who were his friends?

And who was the woman she'd heard him talking to on the telephone that day? Sylvia! Once again, she conjured up visions of a sleek sophisticate, perfectly groomed, probably rich, with that utter confidence society's pampered darlings seem to be born with.

What did she have to offer a man like Ross, who could probably have any woman he wanted? What could he possibly have seen in her? Just a virgin to be seduced? Her cheeks burned at the thought.

"No!" she said aloud, her voice echoing in the empty house. Ross wasn't like that.

When he finally did call, a few nights later, Sarah was so glad to hear the sound of his voice again that all her doubts fled.

"Oh, Ross," she breathed, "I'm so glad you called." Then she forced a lighter tone. "I was beginning to think you might have had another accident."

"No, no, nothing like that," he replied. He sounded distracted, as though his mind were on other things. "I've just been so embroiled in these family and business affairs I've hardly had a moment to think of anything else."

"How is it going?"

"Not well" was the blunt reply. "It's going to be a lot stickier than I thought. It seems there are certain enterprises that will collapse without my supervision, and I'm having a hell of a time convincing them otherwise. The problem is, I do feel a sense of responsibility.''

"Of course. I'm sorry, Ross. I wish I could help."

"You do help," he said in a more intimate tone. "Just by being there. Now, enough of my troubles. What have you been doing? Any new whales on the horizon?"

She told him briefly about the work she'd been doing, and then they said good-night, leaving her with an empty feeling inside. It had been a very unsatisfying conversation. Not one truly personal word. He missed her, but not enough to do anything about it.

She did understand that his business affairs might take time to be worked out, but what about the "unofficial" engagement he'd mentioned? He hadn't brought it up once, and although she was dying to ask him about it, she didn't want him to feel pushed.

From then on, his calls became fewer and farther between. She gave up waiting for the telephone to ring. A week would pass and she'd hear nothing from him. Then when he did call, it was like talking to a stranger. Still, he did keep calling. There were times when she almost wished he wouldn't. Then perhaps she could get on with her life, her work. This limbo was killing her.

In her heart, she believed he really had loved her, perhaps still did, but they had never made any firm plans about the future. There had been no talk of marriage.

She kept telling herself that he was busy, had a lot on his mind, too. It couldn't be easy for him to break from his whole way of life, his family, his work.

Still, the growing anxiety never quite left her. Lying in bed alone at night, staring up at the ceiling, the autumn rains pounding against the windowpane, her mind couldn't let it rest. How long did one telephone call take, just to let her know he was all right and thinking about her?

Had it all been a dream? She began to have serious doubts it had ever happened. She thought about his secrecy, his deceptions and his pretending to be more badly injured than he really was, to gain her sympathy, her trust, depending on her naiveté. Perhaps he and Sylvia were laughing about her together even now, the gullible country girl he'd managed to manipulate into bed.

On a blustery night in late November, Sarah stood at the kitchen window staring out at the phosphorescent waves breaking on the shore. A wind from the north had come up during the day, clearing away the cloud cover, but bringing with it a blast of cold air.

After days of mooning around, unable to work, brooding about Ross's long silence, she knew she had to take some action or go out of her mind. But what could she do?

Should she call him? But how? Everything had happened so fast she hadn't thought to ask for his number, nor he to give it to her. She could always call information. But neither did she have his address. Then she remembered seeing it on his driving license. She squeezed her eyes shut, racking her brain, trying to picture it in her mind. What was it?

Then finally it came to her. Powell Street! That was it. No number, but perhaps the street name was enough. She ran to the telephone, snatched it up and rang the information operator.

It turned out to be far simpler than she'd feared. There was only one Ross Kirk listed on Powell Street in San Francisco. Then quickly, before she could change her mind, she took a deep breath and dialed the number, her heart pounding, but determined now to find out just what was going on. She had to know.

After only a few rings, she heard the receiver being lifted on the other end, then a woman's voice. "Hello?"

For a moment, Sarah was speechless. Then, pulling herself together, she cleared her throat and plunged ahead. "May I please speak to Ross Kirk?" she asked, amazed at how steady her voice was.

"I'm sorry" came the cheerful reply. "Ross is in the shower at the moment. This is Sylvia. Can I take a message?"

"No," Sarah said. "No, thank you. I'll try again another time." Very carefully, she replaced the receiver.

Sylvia! The woman she'd heard him talking to on the telephone that day! Who was she? And what was she doing in Ross's apartment? While he was in the shower? Answering his telephone in the confident, self-assured voice rich, beautiful women seem to be born with?

She gave a start when the shrill ringing of the telephone broke into the stillness of the room. Even though she had virtually given up hope by now, she still felt a little thrill of anticipation. It was his usual time to call. Maybe there was a simple explanation for everything, even the dreaded Sylvia. Quickly, she snatched up the receiver.

But it wasn't Ross. Instead, Timothy's voice came on the line. "Hi, Sarah. How are you?"

"Oh, hello, Timothy," she said, sinking down on the stool. "I'm all right. How about you?"

"Fair to middling" was the hearty reply. "I'm not on duty this weekend and was wondering if you'd like to drive down to Ocean Shores with me and try that new restaurant."

"Oh, Carol and I went there a few weeks ago, and it's not really worth the trip. The prices are horrendous, and the food isn't any better than the Seaside Café in the village."

"I see." There was a short silence. "Well, then, I guess we could always go there. How about it? Would Saturday night suit you?"

She didn't want to go, but anything would be better than sitting in the house alone brooding night after night, waiting for a call that never came.

Then she felt immediately contrite, even ashamed of herself. Timothy might not be the most exciting man in the world, but he'd been a good and loyal friend for years, both to her father and herself. So he was a little dull, a plodder. But then, who wouldn't seem dull compared to Ross, who had swept into her life like a whirlwind?

"Yes, Timothy," she said, putting on a cheerier voice. "That sounds great."

"Good. I'll pick you up around six-thirty. All right?"

She was about to tell him to make it later, in case Ross called, but stopped herself. She couldn't spend the rest of her life sitting around waiting for him.

"That'll be fine, Timothy," she said at last. "I'll be ready."

On Saturday night, she took extra pains to look nice for Timothy. November had swept in like a bear, putting an end to those balmy Indian-summer days of October and bringing with it a cold Arctic wind, constant unremitting rain, and roiling up an angry gray sea.

She wore her dark green woolen dress, one she had bought for her father's funeral, that wouldn't by any stretch of the imagination be considered seductive, but which fitted her slim figure well and flattered her coloring. She fastened on a pair of gold hoop earrings and the thin gold chains that had been her father's last birthday present to her, and stood back from the bedroom mirror to give her reflection one last survey.

Not bad, she thought with satisfaction. Her golden hair hung in loose waves to her shoulders, she'd put on a trace of lip gloss, and although she wouldn't win any beauty contests—or compete with the women in Sylvia's class—she was pleased with her appearance. Just making the effort had also lifted her spirits considerably.

Ross still hadn't called. It had been over a week now, and she had just about resigned herself to the possibility that she'd never hear from him again. Carol had been so right in her warning about getting hurt. She just hadn't realized it would hurt quite this badly.

Still, in her heart of hearts, she believed the experience had been worth it, and although she suffered from the loss, she had no regret that it had happened. To be loved and desired by such a man, even for a short time, was a memory to treasure forever.

Just then the doorbell rang. She glanced at her watch. It was six-thirty on the dot, and she smiled as she turned off the bedroom light and started down the hall for the front door. Leave it to Timothy to be prompt.

Then, just as she passed by the table in the hall where she kept the telephone extension, it rang. She stopped stock-still and stared at it for a few seconds, unable to move, hardly able to breathe. It kept ringing, and in the meantime the doorbell chimed again. What should she do?

She ran to the door and opened it to a beaming Timothy. "Come in," she said in a rush. "Make yourself at home. I just have to answer the telephone."

She left Timothy at the door and ran back to the still-ringing telephone. She stopped a second to catch her breath, then slowly picked up the receiver.

"Hello," she said. Although her heart was pounding wildly, her voice sounded quite calm in her ears.

"Sarah? It's Ross."

Of course she'd known it would be. And with Timothy right there in the living room, able to hear every word!

"Oh, yes," she said pleasantly. "How are you?"

"I'm fine" was the brusque reply. "Listen, Sarah, I'm sorry I haven't called you for a while. I've been tied up in endless conferences with the family, nitpicking over details."

"I see," she said, still quite calm.

For a moment, there was no sound on the line. Then he spoke again, this time with an undercurrent of real concern in his voice. "Sarah? You do understand, don't you?"

"Of course."

"Then what's wrong?"

"Nothing. Nothing at all. How are you feeling? No bad effects from your accident, I hope?"

"Something *is* wrong. Listen, I explained why I haven't called. Are you angry?"

"Oh, no. Only I'm going out to dinner." She laughed. "In fact, you caught me just as we were getting ready to leave."

"I see." There was a long silence. "Timothy, I suppose," he said at last.

"That's right," she replied in a light, cheery voice. "He's waiting for me now in the living room, so I'd better run. Thanks for calling, and I'm glad you're all right."

"What time will you be home?"

"I'm not sure. Probably late."

"Then I'll call again tomorrow. I can see we've got a few things to get straightened out."

"Well, goodbye, then, Ross."

She hung up the telephone and went out to meet Timothy, who was standing awkwardly just inside the door, his face troubled. She went to the hall closet to get her heavy winter coat, then handed it to him so he could help her on with it.

"That was Ross Kirk, I take it," he said quietly behind her as he held the coat for her.

"Yes," she replied, turning around and giving him a warm smile. "He just called to thank me again for taking him in and helping him out when he had that accident."

"I see." He colored slightly and looked down at his feet for a moment, then raised his eyes to hers again. "I know it's probably none of my business, Sarah, and I wasn't eavesdropping, but it seemed to me there was a little more to it than that."

Sarah searched her mind for the right response. She couldn't lie to Timothy, but her feelings about Ross and their future were so nebulous by now that neither did she want to give him the idea there was a serious relationship, either.

"Well," she said at last, choosing her words carefully, "I'll have to admit, as an old friend, that there was a little more while he was here. But I doubt if it's going anywhere."

His brow puckered into a frown, and he opened his mouth as though to admonish her, then snapped it shut and seemed to force out a smile. "Well, it's your life, Sarah. You'll have to deal with it as you think best. But you know how I feel about you. I'll be there for you whenever you need me. Now, shall we get going? I made reservations at the Seaside for seven o'clock."

The dinner with Timothy was a pleasant one, and it did her good to go out, to be with someone who really cared about her, who knew her well enough to leave her alone but still draw her out about her work, and when he left her at the door with a quick brotherly peck on the cheek, she felt better than she had in weeks.

The minute she shut the door on him, the telephone began to ring. She glanced at her watch. It was past ten o'clock. Surely Ross wouldn't be calling her this late. She walked slowly into the hall and picked up the receiver.

"Sarah?" came Ross's peremptory voice. "I've been trying to call you all evening."

"I told you, Ross. I went out to dinner."

"With Timothy."

"Well, yes."

"Listen, I've been thinking. We can't keep on this way. It's ridiculous. I feel you slipping away from me, and you're the one bright spot in this muddled life of mine at the moment. It's time to quit fooling around here, just put an end to it."

Sarah's heart sang. He was coming back to her! It wasn't a dream. "Yes," she said at last, "I agree."

"I've tried my damnedest, but there's no way I can extricate myself down here right now without hurting a lot of other people."

She waited, holding her breath, prepared for him to tell her it was over, that he meant to stay in the life he thought he could leave, and steeling herself to give him up for good.

"But that's no reason why we have to be separated," he went on in a rush, as though he'd had a speech all planned. "So I want you to pack a bag and get on the first plane to San Francisco. I think it would be a good idea for you to get to know something of my life here. You can stay with my sister, Sylvia. She knows all about you and will be delighted to have the company. Now, how soon can you get here?''

CHAPTER SEVEN

Two days later, still in a daze, Sarah boarded a plane at the busy and confusing Seatac Airport in Seattle, settled back in her seat and gazed blankly out the window as the huge jet took off.

It still all seemed unreal. Ross had made the trip sound so plausible on the telephone Saturday night, even necessary. They wanted to be together. Right now, nothing really kept her at the ocean. The autumn migrations were over and wouldn't begin again until spring. She still had the article to finish, but she could do that just as well in San Francisco and had brought along her rough draft to work on.

Now that she was actually on her way, however, the huge jet taxiing down the runway and lifting its nose into the sky, the ground falling away behind them, she had to wonder if she hadn't been out of her mind to agree to go. She was committed now, however. Might as well relax and try to enjoy it. And she would see Ross soon. Then she had to smile. What had really convinced her to go was the fact that the dreaded Sylvia was only his sister!

It was a short trip, just a little over an hour, and before she'd really settled in to enjoy the heady feeling of soaring in the sky over the clouds, they were already landing in San Francisco. It was dark out by this time, the lights of the city and the two graceful bridges twinkling against the night sky.

As she trailed along with the other debarking passengers into the busy, noisy and confusing terminal, she searched the crowd for some sign of Ross, craning her neck, her eyes moving over the hordes of people milling about, feeling just like an ant that had strayed from its hill.

Then she saw him. Since he was several inches taller than most of the other men, he was actually hard to miss. He was coming toward her, weaving his way through the crowd, one hand raised in greeting, his face wreathed in a broad, welcoming smile.

"Sarah!" he called. "Over here."

For a moment, she could only stand there staring at him. He looked wonderful, still tanned from his stay at the beach, his face alight with pleasure. Over a dark gray suit and tie, he was wearing a tan trench coat. How could she ever even have considered not coming? Her one regret was that the only decent thing she had to wear for the trip was her old navy blue suit. There hadn't been time for shopping. But this was San Francisco! Surely she could pick up more suitable clothing. She'd brought all the cash she could lay her hands on at such short notice for just that purpose after all.

Just then she spotted an opening in the crowd. She broke through it and began to hurry toward him. When she reached him, he put his hands on her shoulders and gazed down at her, the love and joy on his face unmistakable.

Yet, as she gave him a closer look, she could see the shadow in his eyes, the lines at the corners creased more deeply, the faint dark smudges below them, the pallor beneath the tan. He looked exhausted, and her heart went out to him.

"So," he said. "You did come."

She laughed. "Did you really doubt I would?"

"Well, I did have my moments," he admitted with a shake of his head. "You didn't sound too thrilled with the idea when I suggested it over the telephone the other night."

"I'm here now," she replied, gazing up happily into his eyes. "So you're stuck with me."

"Oh, I think I can handle that," he said. He put an arm around her shoulders and began to lead her toward the escalator. "Now, let's pick up your luggage and head for Sylvia's place. She has dinner waiting."

Sarah's heart quailed. Her luggage! One shabby suitcase, stuffed with the only clothes she owned that might conceivably pass muster in this strange new world. Even her underwear was worn and needed replacement, and she vowed that the first thing she'd do was go on a shopping spree. She didn't want Ross to be ashamed of her. She was in his world now and wanted desperately to live up to it.

After they collected her suitcase, they walked together through a light drizzle, more fog than rain, to the parking area. Ross carried her suitcase with one hand and kept his other arm around her, holding her close, as though realizing she needed that security in this new alien environment.

"You'll really like Sylvia," he said, as they walked toward his car. "And she's anxious to meet you." He laughed. "She's been trying to marry me off for years, and is dying to get a look at the one woman in the world who could convince me.''

Sarah's heart soared even higher. It was the first time he'd mentioned marriage. Although it wasn't exactly a proposal, it did sound as though he simply took it for granted.

They had reached the car by now, a sleek, dark gray Mercedes, and while he stowed her bag in the back, she settled herself in front and waited for him.

''I take it Sylvia is the sister you battled with as a child, then grew close to later on,'' she remarked when he'd gotten inside.

''Yes,'' he replied shortly. ''But let's not talk about that now.'' He moved closer to her and put a hand on her face. ''I'm so glad you've come, Sarah,'' he said in a low voice. ''I never realized just how much I missed you until I saw you coming down that ramp tonight. You're like a breath of fresh air in this crazy world I've found myself entangled in.''

She smiled into his eyes. ''Well, we'll just have to untangle you, then, won't we?''

''You can do it, if anyone can,'' he said.

With a low noise deep in his throat, he reached out for her and enfolded her in his arms, clutching at her almost roughly, as though afraid she'd vanish if he didn't hang on. He held her like that for a few moments, gazing deeply down into her eyes.

Then, as his head bent toward hers, she closed her eyes, waiting for his kiss. When it came, it was full of urgency, his mouth pulling greedily at hers, as though to suck the life out of her, and she returned it with all her heart.

He shifted his body so that he was facing her, his weight forcing her backward, the kiss deepening as his tongue pushed past her lips to fill her mouth. His hand slipped under her coat and moved to her breast, sliding sensuously over the thin material of her silk shirt and sending fireworks off in her head.

"Oh, Sarah," he breathed into her ear. "How I want you!"

Then he stiffened and pulled back from her, his hands moving to her shoulders. In the dim glow coming from the tall light standards surrounding the area, she could just make out his flushed face, the little muscles twitching along his jawline, and knew the effort he was making to control himself.

"If this place wasn't so public..." he muttered grimly.

She laughed and straightened up. "My, that was quite a welcome," she said lightly, and could hear the crack in her voice. "But we probably should get going, don't you think?"

"Yes, I suppose so." He turned to start the engine, then glanced over at her when it caught. "But you'll never know how close you came to being ravished right here in the front seat of my car."

The traffic was heavy that night, slowed even further by the constant drizzle, which now had become a real downpour, so they drove along in silence until they climbed a steep hill and turned into the gate of what looked like a park filled with trees and shrubbery and surrounded by a tall wrought-iron fence. They drove slowly down a curved driveway to the front of a large, imposing-looking house.

Ross pulled up in front of it, switched off the engine and turned to her. "Well, here we are. Home sweet home."

She gazed at him blankly. "But you don't live here."

"No. I have my own place. Sylvia stayed in the family home when the rest of us moved on. In fact, she's kept house for my father ever since my mother died."

"Then she never married?"

He frowned. "Once, some time ago. But it didn't take." He opened his door. "Well, shall we go?"

She turned to give the house a closer look, her heart sinking within her. It was far more affluent than she'd ever imagined, with a wide stone staircase leading up to the entrance, flanked by a low balustrade, with concrete urns filled with flowers on either side. How could she ever hope to fit into such a milieu?

She turned back to Ross. "I suppose we might as well get it over with," she said in a small voice.

After one look, he seemed to sense her misgivings and pulled her to him. "Darling," he said in a low, soothing voice, "there's absolutely nothing to be nervous about. They'll all love you as much as I do. You'll see."

She reared her head back and gazed up at him in horror. "All? What do you mean by all? I thought it was just going to be Sylvia."

He shrugged and gave her a sheepish smile. "Well, my father does live here, you know. And when the others found out you were coming tonight, wild horses couldn't keep them from coming over to meet you." He gave her a little shake. "Come on, now, it'll be all right. I'll be with you every step of the way."

The rest of that evening passed in a whirl of confusion. Later, alone in the sanctuary of her own room, Sarah vaguely recalled meeting what seemed like hundreds of people, all strange to her, but which actually only comprised Ross's immediate family.

There were Sylvia and their father—she could keep them straight, at least—but then there were his brother, the doctor, and his wife and children, and the other sister and her husband and children. She couldn't even remember their names, couldn't even recall eating at all, except for pushing around what was probably a wonderful meal on her plate while trying to keep a stupid smile plastered on her face as she watched the family in action.

Although she could tell that Ross was making a valiant effort to stay by her side and help her through the ordeal, even he seemed to be absorbed back into his family's particular ambiance when they all were together. For an only child like Sarah, living a largely solitary life, it had all been too much.

Finally, at some point during dessert, Sylvia, a stylish dark-haired matronly woman, rose majestically to her feet and simply announced that she was taking Sarah to her room, and the rest of the family could either go home or talk to each other. Ross, embroiled in a heated discussion with his brother, had jumped to his feet, guilt written all over his face, and pulled her chair back for her.

"I'll take her," he announced to his sister. "Where are you putting her?"

"No," Sylvia declared in imperious tones. "You can see her tomorrow. Right now, she needs to be alone." Then she looked at Sarah, her stern expression softened into a smile. "Right, Sarah?"

Before Sarah even had a chance to answer, Sylvia strode to her side, took her by the arm and marched her up the wide, curving staircase to the upper story, chatting all the way about the original Kirks who had built the house after the great earthquake.

The bedroom was luxurious beyond Sarah's wildest expectations, yet in a subdued way. No frills, no dramatics, but obviously furnished and decorated with an eye to lasting, a feminine room, with deep, rose-colored draperies and bedspread, thick white carpet, solid mahogany furniture in a graceful Queen Anne style, and delicate floral watercolors hung on the rose-and-white-striped walls.

"Sorry about the family," Sylvia announced gruffly when she ushered Sarah inside. "I tried to convince them you needed to be alone your first night here, but it's like talking to the wind when they have their minds made up. At any rate, I'm very glad you're here." She hesitated a moment, then went on more slowly. "You see, with all his faults, I love my brother very much. I think he's been very unhappy for a long time now, but when he came back from your place, he was like a changed man." She cleared her throat loudly. "But we can talk about that later. Right now, I'll leave you alone. Sleep well, and if you need anything, you'll find me in the library.''

With that, she turned and left the room, closing the door quietly behind her. When she was gone, Sarah just stood in the middle of the enormous room, her head whirling, a deep lassitude gripping her. It was all too much for her. Then she noticed that there was an adjoining bathroom, with tiles in the same rose-and-white color scheme as the bedroom.

A bath! she thought. A long, relaxing soak. Then fall into bed, get a good night's sleep. Tomorrow things would surely sort themselves out.

But she slept fitfully that night, waking several times to the strange noises of the city, a siren blaring on its way to some disaster or other, the distant clanging of a cable car, the deep hoot of a foghorn out on the bay, the constant traffic going by the house.

To while away the sleepless hours, she lay there in the dark, wide-eyed, staring up at the ceiling and trying to picture the members of Ross's family she had met that evening at dinner, to sort them out in her mind. But except for Sylvia and their father, the rest were only a blur.

The one thing that was etched indelibly in her memory was the fact that every single one of the other women present was dressed and groomed to perfection. Beautiful, expensive clothes, perfect subdued makeup, tasteful jewelry, simple—and costly—coiffures and manicures. She thought of her own shabby clothes, the unstyled blond hair, still streaked from the summer sun, the fingernails

cut almost to the quick for ease in working, and
was overwhelmed with a sense of abject inadequacy.

She simply *must* at least buy some new clothes,
get her hair styled. She didn't want Ross to be
ashamed of her.

As it turned out, however, she didn't get the chance
to do any shopping in the next few days. Ross appeared the next morning soon after breakfast, and
Sylvia tactfully made her exit, leaving them alone
in the immense breakfast room.

"Well?" he said, taking a seat across from her
and pouring coffee out for himself from the solid
silver pot into one of Sylvia's delicate china cups.
"How did you sleep last night?"

"Oh, all right," she said, forcing out a smile.

He gave her a close look. "Yes, I can tell," he
remarked dryly. "You look as though you've been
up all night."

She laughed and ran a hand through her hair.
"Well, thanks a lot! That's just what a girl wants
to hear so early in the morning."

"Early!" he exclaimed, glancing at his watch.
"It's almost ten o'clock. And I have big plans for
the day. First, I thought I'd take you to the
Embarcadero. Then you really must have a ride on
the cable car. We can have lunch out at Seal Rock,
take a run through Golden Gate Park, maybe visit
Fleischacker's Zoo, if you like, have tea at the
Japanese garden—"

"Hey, slow down!" she cried, laughing and
holding up a hand. "I've barely arrived and you're
already sweeping me off my feet. I really wanted
to do some shopping."

"Oh, shopping," he said, waving a hand dismissively in the air. "You can always go shopping. I've arranged my schedule—not without enormous opposition, I might add—to spend the next few days with you. So let me play host and show you the sights. And," he went on, lowering his voice and giving her a look full of meaning, "I want to show you where I live. This house is far too public with the family constantly in and out for what's on my mind."

All Sarah's resistance melted at that look, that intimate tone, the implication of his words. Who cared if she looked like the shabby country cousin compared to the sophisticated women in Ross's family? Who needed new clothes? Ross wanted her, loved her, desired her, just the way she was.

"Well," she said, cocking her head to one side and giving him a mischievous look, "we'll see about that. I'm not sure I should trust you."

He threw back his head and laughed. "Oh, you can trust me all right! And you know exactly what for."

For the first time since she'd arrived, he looked more like the old Ross she remembered from those happy days at the beach. His color was better, the shadow was gone from his eyes, alight now with the old gray gleam, and the lines on his forehead and around his eyes seemed to have smoothed out somewhat.

If my coming here can do that for him, she thought, then it's all worthwhile.

After a morning of sight-seeing, they stopped for lunch at an elegant restaurant high on a cliff overlooking Seal Rock. The ocean pounding against the rugged shore reminded Sarah of home and made the city seem less strange, less forbidding.

"What I want to know," she said over their pre-lunch glass of wine, "is why you looked so tired last night when you picked me up at the airport."

He gave her a startled look. "Did I?" he asked. "Look tired, that is?"

She nodded firmly. "Yes. Definitely. What is it, Ross? Something's troubling you, I can tell."

All morning, as hard as he tried to act light-hearted and as if he were enjoying himself, there were times when she would catch an expression on his face, a distracted look, his mind seeming to be a million miles away, fastened on something that profoundly disturbed him.

He gazed past her, frowning, for a few moments. "I'm sorry," he said at last, turning back to her. "I didn't know it showed."

"To me, it does," she said softly.

He took a long, slow swallow of his wine. Then, as though having made up his mind, he put his elbows on the table and leaned across it toward her, a look of grim determination on his face.

"The truth is," he began carefully, "that I can't seem to get unstuck here no matter how hard I try. In fact, the harder I do try the more deeply I seem to dig myself in. By the time I put out one fire, settle one burning issue, another one has sprung up behind me."

"Tell me about it," she said quietly. "All the gory details."

He began speaking slowly, haltingly at first, then as he warmed to his subject, with an earnestness that told her just how desperate he was. She'd already known that he'd left on his solitary trip to the northwest coast to sort out his future, to decide what he really wanted to do with the rest of his life, but now, for the first time, he explained what it was he was trying to escape, and why it was so difficult.

"What they want me to do is take over the running of all the family business enterprises," he said. "It's really my father who's putting the pressure on me, using every trick in the book to convince me. He plays on my sympathy, claims he's getting too old to do the job, throws the family honor and integrity up to me, even threatens me with disinheritance if I refuse."

"And what do *you* want?" she asked when he fell silent.

He heaved an exasperated sigh. "At this point, I'm not sure. When I left here a few months ago, I thought I knew. Then when I met you, fell in love with you, it seemed quite clear. But the truth is, what else *can* I do? I've been groomed all my life to take over from my father. My brother is wrapped up in his medicine, as he should be. My sisters' husbands are a big help in the business, but aren't cut out to run things, don't even want to."

The waiter came to take their order just then, and while Ross discussed the menu and the wine list with him, Sarah mulled over all the things Ross had told her.

"So," Ross said, when the waiter had left, "that's pretty much the situation. If I chuck it all, just go off and beachcomb or study whales with you, I abandon responsibilities I've always been expected to take, leave my family in the lurch. If I stay here and do what they want, I feel I'm giving up my one chance at happiness. I'm damned if I do, damned if I don't.''

The note of hopelessness in his voice struck a deep chord in Sarah. "Well, it seems quite clear to me," she said slowly at last.

"Oh, really?" he asked with a wry twist of his mouth. "Tell me about it."

"You have to do what will make you able to live with yourself, even if it means a sacrifice of what you want—or what you feel is expected of you, either way. If you stay, you give up something precious to you. But if you chuck it all, perhaps you'd be giving up something even more precious. Your sense of honor and integrity."

He frowned. "If you're saying what I think you're saying, you think I should stick it out here, take up the cudgels and do my duty."

"No. I'm not saying that at all. Only you can decide what you can or can't live with. I'm only guessing that in the end you might decide against having your own way. But again, only you know the answer."

"And what about us? You're the one bright spot in the whole mess. Nothing would be worth losing you. What do *you* want?"

She'd been so absorbed in helping Ross resolve his personal dilemma that she hadn't considered her own stake in his decision. What *did* she want? The answer was clear. She wanted him to leave all the glitter behind, to come to the beach and live with her, simply, freely. But she wanted a whole Ross even more.

"I love you," she said quietly at last. "If that means getting used to living in your world, then that's what I'll do."

"And what about your own work? Your life?"

"You *are* my life now, Ross," she said.

After a superb lunch of fresh seafood, a mélange of lobster, crab and mussels baked in a delicate wine sauce, they took a stroll down the precipitous path to the edge of the cliff to walk off some of the enormous meal.

The perennial San Francisco morning fog had burned off by this time, and down below, on one huge flat boulder, a sleek gray seal was warming itself in the late-autumn sun, now high overhead. They stood there in silence for some time, watching, then Ross put his arm around her and drew her more closely to his side.

"Does it make you homesick?" he asked. "The sea?"

She smiled up into his face. "Not really. It's the same ocean after all. Besides, I just got here last night. I haven't had time to get homesick yet." She'd always feel at home, she thought, with Ross by her side.

"Well, what now?" he asked. "Do you feel like more sight-seeing? There's still a lot to do."

She laughed. "Not really. To tell you the truth, a good nap is what sounds best to me right now. I'm rather tired."

He nodded. "Fair enough." He hesitated for a moment, then went on in a more sober voice. "But before I take you back to Sylvia's, I'd like to make one stop."

"Ah. Business?" she asked.

"Oh, no. Not today. But I do want to show you where I live."

The glint deep in the gray eyes, the tightening of his hold on her, the softness of his tone, all told her just what he had in mind, and a heated glow began to spread through her.

"Yes," she said, "I'd like that."

As they drove through the city streets toward his home, Ross pointed out various landmarks—both bridges, of course, Mount Tamalpais, Coit Tower, the busy waterfront—until he started up a steep hill in a quiet residential district.

"These are all old mansions," he explained, gesturing at the huge houses that lined both sides of the narrow street. "They've mostly been converted into condominiums." He pulled up in the middle of the block. "And this one is where I live. In fact, the family owns the building. I have the whole ground floor, so it's quite roomy. More space than I need, really."

They got out of the car and walked up the flagstone path toward a private entrance, sheltered by dense shrubbery. Ross unlocked the door, then held it open for her, and Sarah stepped inside a wide foyer that was as big as the whole studio Ross had stayed in at the beach.

She stood there speechless, goggling, taking in the graceful antique table along the wall, the paintings above it, the fresh flowers in the beautiful porcelain vase sitting on top.

"Come on," he said, locking the door behind him and taking her by the arm. "I'll give you the grand tour."

He led her through one beautiful room after another, a sitting room with a formal Adam fireplace, a library filled with books and the clutter of business, a dining room that would seat twelve easily, powder room, guest bedroom and bath, all decorated tastefully, expensively, and in a decidedly masculine fashion.

They had reached the end of a long hallway now, the door shut. Ross put his hand on the knob, pushed it open, then turned to her.

"And this is my room," he said.

She turned to face him, suddenly shy, to see that he was gazing down deeply into her eyes, a questioning look in the gray depths. "But before we go inside, I want you to know that you hold all the cards here." His voice took on a gruffer tone. "There can't be any doubt in your mind how badly I want you right now, have wanted you every day since I left you at the beach. But I know what kind of woman you are. If you'd rather wait..." His voice trailed off.

She gave him a puzzled look. "Wait? I don't understand. Wait for what?"

His eyes widened. "Why, until we're married, of course."

So, there it was, out in the open again. Obviously, he'd intended it all along, just hadn't felt it necessary to make a formal proposal or declaration.

Then he frowned. "You *do* want to marry me, don't you, Sarah? Maybe I've been taking too much for granted here. I mean, I just assumed you never would have—"

"Oh, Ross!" she broke in, laughing, her own tension vanquished at the sight of his discomfiture. "Of course I want to marry you."

"Well, that's all right, then," he said, clearly relieved. "The problem is that the way things are so unsettled now with the business, the family, I don't feel we should set a date, or even announce an official engagement. That's why I've held off trying to make any definite plans. You do see, don't you, darling? I've got to get things settled here before I can take on the responsibility of a wife, hopefully a family."

"Yes," she said slowly, "I guess so. But it seems to me you might be waiting for something that may never happen. I mean, life doesn't work out that way. You can't wait until you have everything neatly pigeonholed, every detail settled, before doing what you really want to do."

A troubled frown creased his forehead, and he set his jaw in the unyielding line that was so familiar to her. Alarmed, she began to panic. The one thing she did *not* want, at all costs, was to lose him. He'd said she held all the cards, but that wasn't quite true.

"Ross, I'm sorry," she went on hastily. "You know best what you have to do about your family, your business." She took a deep breath, then reached out a hand to place it on his cheek, forcing him around to face her again. "And the answer is no."

A ghost of a smile played around his lips. "No what?"

"No, I don't want to wait."

He stared at her silently for a fraction of a second, then, with a low groan deep in his throat, threw his arms around her and held her to him. As they stood there, bodies pressed together, Sarah could feel his hard need pressing against her thigh, the heat building up between them like a continuing charge of electricity.

His mouth was at her ear now, and she could feel his labored breath. "I do love you, darling," he murmured. "And I'll never do anything to hurt you. You know that, don't you?"

"Yes," she said in a muffled voice, "I do. And I love you, too. With all my heart."

His lips sought hers then, in a kiss of such tenderness and sweetness that her last lingering doubt was vanquished, and she threw her arms around his neck, running her hands through the thick dark hair, all shyness and reserve abandoned in the sheer joy of being held in the arms of the man she loved.

As the kiss deepened, became more urgent, his hands slid under her suit jacket and began to move feverishly over her back, then around to settle on her breasts. Slowly, gradually, he began to tug at her clothes, first the jacket, which fell to the floor unheeded, then, as they moved, still locked together, into the bedroom, her blouse and skirt followed, until she stood before him by the side of the bed, dressed only in her slip.

When he had removed his own jacket and shirt, she reached out impulsively to run her hands over the smooth flesh of his broad muscled chest, his flat abdomen, ending at the thin line of black hair that trailed beneath the waistband of his trousers, hovering slightly there.

Slowly, he pulled the straps of her slip over her shoulders and down her hips, then slid his hands up the full length of her body, stopping at her bare breasts, covering them, stroking, brushing his fingers lightly over them, each new touch sending shafts of fire through her. The dark head came down to her breast then, his lips and tongue playing with one throbbing peak, then the other, and she threw her head back, lost in a mindless surrender.

Suddenly, he swooped her up in his arms and carried her to the side of the bed. He set her down gently on top of it, then stood gazing at her, his eyes glowing with love and desire. Quickly, he removed his trousers and lay down beside her, enfolding her once again in his arms, his hands stroking, his mouth nuzzling every inch of her bare body, until finally, hovering above her, his glittering gray eyes never leaving eyes, he carried her with him over the edge.

CHAPTER EIGHT

ALTHOUGH Ross had to get back to work after those first few blissful days alone with him, days he had devoted entirely to her, he did manage to call her at least once during the day, just to chat and check on how she was getting along.

They also had dinner together every evening, either with the family at Sylvia's, or out at yet another of San Francisco's fine restaurants, or, best of all, putting together a scratch meal at his place.

She soon got the rest of the family sorted out, and although she felt most comfortable with Sylvia, the others did seem to be going out of their way to make her feel welcome. She saw, too, how they all looked up to Ross, depended on him to hold the business and the family together, and realized why he found it so difficult to extricate himself.

His father especially relied on him. He was a rather distant man, clearly as strong-willed as his son, and still active. But as Sarah observed him more closely, she could see that he had frailties he wasn't quite able to hide from his family—forgetfulness, a slight tremor in his hands, a tendency to drift off to sleep during dinner.

In the meantime, she did her best to adapt to Ross's world. With each passing day, it became clearer to her that it was going to be far more difficult than she'd dreamed—if not impossible—for

him to break away, no matter how much he longed
to do so.

One gray gloomy morning two weeks after her ar-
rival, she was sitting in the breakfast room with
Sylvia when the telephone rang on the sideboard.
Sylvia reached out a hand to answer it, then handed
it to Sarah with a knowing smile. "Here, it's for
you," she said, then rose to her feet and tactfully
left the room.

"Good morning" came Ross's voice when she'd
answered. "I just called to tell you I have to go out
of town for a few days on business. Will you be all
right?"

"Of course," she said with a laugh. "I can get
my shopping done. Where are you going? How long
will you be gone?"

"Just down to Los Angeles, and I'm not sure for
how long. We're negotiating the purchase of a small
electronics company, and those things can drag on
for days. I'll call you, though, and let you know
how things go. I have to run now to catch my
plane."

"Well, goodbye, then. I'll miss you." But he had
already hung up, and when she found herself
speaking to dead air, she slowly replaced the
receiver.

She got up from the table and went to the window
that overlooked the back garden, with its wide
flagstone terrace, immaculate lawn and the late
roses still in bloom. She couldn't get used to the
sight of blooming flowers in December. They
looked sad somehow, and rather gloomy in the fine
mist that covered everything.

Buck up now, my girl, she told herself firmly. So he's going to be gone for a few days. No reason to fall into a blue funk. Still, a little nagging voice deep within her whispered insistently that she wished he'd asked her to go along with him. But that was silly. He'd be too busy.

She sighed heavily and was turning back to pour herself another cup of coffee when Sylvia poked her head inside.

"All clear?" she asked.

"Yes."

"Well, that was short—and sweet, I hope," Sylvia said, coming into the room. Then she gave Sarah a closer look. "Is something wrong? You look like you've just heard dreadful news."

Sarah forced out a smile. "Oh, no. Not really. Ross just called to tell me he'll be out of town for a few days. In Los Angeles, on business." When she heard the wistful note in her own voice, she laughed lightly to cover it up. "Actually, it's just as well. I've wanted to do some shopping."

"It seems to me he could have taken you with him," Sylvia commented dryly.

Sarah shrugged. "Oh, well. He'll probably be too busy to spend much time with me anyway."

Sylvia crossed over to the table and slowly poured coffee into her cup, her expression thoughtful, a frown creasing her forehead. Then, as though having made up her mind to face a thorny ordeal, she straightened up, took a sip of coffee and gave Sarah a direct look.

"I realize it's none of my business, Sarah, and you can tell me to get stuffed if I'm trespassing on forbidden territory, but I assume you and Ross are talking marriage.''

"Well, yes," Sarah replied carefully. "But there's nothing official about it yet. He feels he has to get his position in the family business sorted out first.''

Sylvia nodded. "And of course, everything naturally hinges on what *he* wants." She gave an exasperated sigh. "I've found that men have a very nasty habit of charming the socks off a woman to get what they want from her, then ignoring her once they get it. It's one reason I never married again after the first one flopped.''

Sarah reddened. ''Well, I'm afraid I wouldn't know much about that subject.''

Sylvia stared at her, narrow-eyed, for a long time, and it was all Sarah could do to keep from squirming in her chair. How could she tell Sylvia that she'd never even been in love before? She felt like some kind of freak.

Finally, Sylvia smiled, reached out a hand to place it over Sarah's and gave it a squeeze. "I must say, I envy you your luck first time out. Ross is a fine man, even if he is my brother." She made a face. "Mine was a real rat.''

As it turned out, Ross was gone almost a week. It only took Sarah one afternoon to get her shopping done, and when she got home and saw what she'd bought, she was appalled. All she'd done was duplicate the clothes she already had—sensible cotton shirtwaisters, denim pants, tailored blouses, one very plain blue woolen dress.

She missed Ross terribly, and the results of her shopping spree didn't help improve her spirits. How could she hope to fit into his life if she fell into a panic every time he had to go out of town on business, and didn't even have enough clothes sense to dress the part expected of her as the wife of an important executive?

She thought of Sylvia and the other women in the family, all dressed beautifully, even in their most casual clothes. Perhaps she could ask one of them to help her. But Sylvia was so busy, running the house, on the board of several charities and caught up in a whirl of social affairs that seemed to consume every spare moment of her day. The others were so wrapped up with their growing families that they didn't seem to have much free time, either.

When Ross did come back, he called her first thing, and when they went out to dinner that night, he seemed glad to see her, was as loving as ever, but there was an air of abstraction about him, a new distance between them that troubled her.

"So, how did it go in Los Angeles?" she asked over cocktails. "Did you manage to put out the fire?"

"No," he said shortly, a shadow crossing his face. "It's going to be much more difficult than I thought. I'm sorry, Sarah, but it looks as though I'll be spending more time in Los Angeles than I'd counted on. In fact, I have to go back tomorrow. I only came back to pick up some documents I need. And," he added, his face softening, "to see you."

"I see," she said carefully. She gazed down at her glass, twisting it around in the napkin, then raised her eyes to his. "I don't suppose it would work out for me to go with you?" she asked.

"Darling, there's nothing I'd like better," he said, reaching across the table to take her hand in his. "But I'm afraid you'd be bored out of your mind. I'm tied up in meetings most days from breakfast until late at night. We really would hardly see any more of each other than we do now."

"Yes, of course. I understand."

Ross came back from Los Angeles on schedule, and they did have one glorious evening together. But he had to leave again the next day, and as she said goodbye to him that night, it dawned on her that a pattern had already set in, one she'd just have to learn to live with, like it or not.

When he was with her, he still seemed abstracted. Even his lovemaking was more perfunctory, less ardent. She tried to get him to talk about his work, but he always brushed her questions aside with a frown, as though he needed to keep his working and personal lives separate. It was almost as though the man she'd fallen in love with at the beach was slowly disappearing.

This went on for the next few weeks. She had told him she understood his long absences, his silences, but she didn't, really. What did he expect her to do with herself while he was gone? She didn't know anyone except his family, and they had their own lives to live. She took long walks, traveled around the city on public transportation, got a lot of reading done, but one empty day seemed to stretch in front of another, and she found herself missing her old home, her friends, her far simpler life, where she had her own work to do and could be herself.

As she sat all alone in Sylvia's vast formal sitting room one dreary afternoon, brooding, sudden tears began to sting behind her eyes, and she let them fall unchecked. She was homesick! She'd told Ross her home was with him, but when he was gone so much of the time, what was there for her here?

Just then, Sylvia burst inside, her face red with the sudden cold snap that had settled in recently. "Brr," she said, rubbing her hands together and shedding her coat. "It's freezing out there."

Then she gave Sarah a sharp look. Although she'd tried to hide her tears the minute she heard Sylvia come inside, she knew it was too late.

"Sarah!" Sylvia cried, rushing to her side. "You've been crying. What is it?"

"Oh, nothing, really. Just a bout of home-sickness, I guess."

Sylvia eyed her carefully for a few moments. "Listen, my dear," she said at last. "I've pretty much left you alone since you've been here. Somehow I had the impression that's what you wanted. But now, with Ross gone so much of the time, we'd better start thinking about launching you into society."

Sarah gave her a stricken look. "Oh, I couldn't, Sylvia. Not without Ross. I'd feel like a fish out of water."

"Well, Ross isn't here, is he?" Sylvia demanded shortly. "So what do you intend to do after you're married? Sit around all day and wait for him to come home?"

"I don't know," Sarah said miserably. "I just didn't think at all, I guess." Then she raised her chin. "And I'm still not that sure Ross intends to stay here."

Sylvia's eyes widened. "But of course he'll stay! What else would he do? This is his life. We all depend on him. He'd never let the family down. Oh, I guess he did have some harebrained idea once of leaving. But I chalked that up to an early mid-life crisis. I knew he'd get over it. And I'm convinced he has. So now you have to consider what it is you want."

She seemed so certain of her belief that Sarah had to take it seriously. And if she was right, where did that leave her? What did she want? That was easy. She wanted Ross. Then, little by little, something began to stir inside her. She'd been behaving like a spoiled child, refusing to play the game just because Ross seemed to be neglecting her. As the wife of a busy executive, she'd have to get used to that, if she wanted to keep him.

"You're right," she said at last. "I guess in my heart I just kept hoping that maybe..." She shrugged. "But I see now I was wrong. So, will you help me?"

Sylvia sat down beside her. "Of course I'll help you. I've been dying to get my hand in, if the truth were known." She leaned back, put her chin in her hand and gave Sarah a long, careful scrutiny. "I don't want to hurt your feelings," she said at last, "but we really should start with your clothes and hair."

Sarah nodded eagerly. "Yes. I think you're right."

"And there's an important party coming up next weekend. A charity ball at the Van Ness home."

She gave a knowing smile. "I'm sure Ross mentioned their daughter, Laura. The Van Nesses are close business associates and old family friends. In fact, we all expected Laura and Ross would marry eventually." She laughed. "Especially Laura, I might add." Then she added quickly, "But he chose you, Sarah. Don't ever forget that. Now, where shall we start?"

For the next week, every minute Sylvia could spare from her busy schedule she devoted to Sarah. They shopped for clothes at some of San Francisco's most exclusive stores, and while Sarah had to repress a shudder at the money she was spending, she finally convinced herself it was all in a good cause, even what her father might have wanted her to do with her inheritance.

She had her hair styled in a more sophisticated upsweep, and since she'd let her fingernails grow, the professional manicure did wonders for her hands. She spent hours in a luxurious salon learning how to use the myriad jars, bottles, tubes and boxes of makeup she'd purchased, and even had a scent, musky and seductive, chosen for her.

The gown they'd chosen for the formal ball coming up that weekend was a vision of the palest aquamarine, the color so faint as to appear almost white, setting off the remainder of her summer tan nicely. When they came home from shopping that day, Sylvia insisted she model it for her again outside the hectic confines of the shop.

In her bedroom, after she'd put it on, Sarah stood in front of the full-length mirror, staring at the apparition she saw there as though looking at a stranger. The new hairstyle made her look older, less girlish, the makeup more sophisticated. But it was the dress that made her catch her breath.

The neckline of the silk bodice plunged so low that even the filmy tulle covering it did little to hide the deep cleavage between her firm, full breasts. She could never wear it in public. What had possessed her to buy it? It was Sylvia's fault, she thought with more than a touch of resentment. She'd talked her into it.

Just then, Sylvia herself appeared at the door, rapping lightly on it. "Ready?" she called as she stepped inside. "I'm dying to see how it looks...."

She stopped short, staring at Sarah's reflection, and when Sarah turned around to face her, she uttered a long sigh. "My dear," she said, walking toward her, "you look absolutely sensational."

"Sylvia, I cannot wear this dress. It's too..." She couldn't finish, at a loss for words.

"What? Are you out of your mind? It's a wonderful dress. If I had the figure for it, I'd snatch it off your back and wear it myself. Don't be silly. You're in the big city now. Women wear that kind of thing all the time. Just wait and see. Trust me."

"Well..." Sarah said, weakening.

Sylvia patted her on the shoulder and gave her an encouraging smile. "It'll be fine. Don't worry. Now," she said, turning to go, "I have to see about dinner. Oh, and by the way, I suppose Ross already mentioned to you that he'll be able to make the party." She laughed. "I made him swear his most sacred oath."

Sarah stared at her. "Oh, is he back?"

"Yes. Came home yesterday. Hasn't he called you?"

"No," Sarah replied numbly.

"Not to worry," Sylvia said, grinning broadly. "You were probably out getting beautified when he called. Just wait until he sees you in that dress, that hairstyle. He won't be able to keep his hands off you."

Ross did call her later that evening. Although she'd felt hurt, even angry, that he hadn't let her know he was back sooner, she was so glad to hear the sound of his voice her annoyance evaporated quickly.

"Where in the world have you been?" he demanded the minute she answered the telephone. "I tried to call you yesterday and no one answered."

The glow she felt was only slightly dampened by the fact that he could have tried again. "Oh, I finally got my shopping done."

"That's good. I'm afraid I'm tied up in meetings until God knows when, so I won't be able to see you tonight. How about coming down to the office tomorrow and having lunch with me? I've got to go back to Los Angeles later in the day, so it'll be the only chance we'll have to see each other."

"Yes, fine. I can do that. But you are going to make it back for the ball this Saturday, aren't you?"

"Oh, yes" was the grim reply. "Those affairs aren't exactly my idea of having fun, but it's virtually a command performance. Besides, that's business, too, in a way, since the Van Ness family and ours have close ties within the company."

*   *   *

The offices of Kirk Enterprises were housed in a medium-size building in the heart of the financial district named, impressively, the Kirk Building.

The reception area itself was plush, with a wide foyer carpeted in thick beige carpet and what looked like genuine Oriental rugs placed strategically. The furniture appeared to be antique, and there were original oil paintings, landscapes mostly, on the walls, with one very impossible-looking portrait of a man who looked very much like Ross and must be an ancestor of some kind.

She'd worn one of her new purchases, a trim black woolen suit with a frothy silk-and-lace blouse underneath, a pair of wickedly high-heeled black shoes, and as she approached the sleek, dark-haired receptionist behind the fragile-looking mahogany desk, the new clothes and hairstyle seemed to give her courage.

"Yes?" the young woman asked, giving her a frosty look.

"I'm Sarah Wainwright, here to see Ross Kirk."

"Oh, yes, Miss Wainwright," she cried, smiling and jumping up from her chair. "I'll just let him know you're here. Would you like a cup of coffee? Tea? Please do sit down. It'll only be a moment."

"Nothing, thanks," Sarah replied, amazed at the impact her name obviously had on the woman and certain that she wouldn't have received such deference if she'd come to these elegant offices looking like Miss Country Mouse.

In just a few moments, a pleasant-looking, fortyish, gray-haired woman, dressed as expensively as Sarah herself, appeared walking toward her, holding out a hand.

"Miss Wainwright?" she said with a smile. "I'm Janet Patterson, Mr. Kirk's secretary. It's so good to meet you. Now, if you'll just come with me, I'll show you to his room."

Warmed by the friendly welcome, Sarah went with her down a long corridor lined with offices, where every occupant seemed to be speaking urgently into a telephone, to the very end, where Janet stopped in front of a massive carved double door and knocked smartly.

"Come in," called Ross's familiar voice.

With a smile, the secretary pushed open the door, stood aside for Sarah to enter, then turned and walked smartly back down the hall, her footsteps muffled in the heavy carpet.

Ross was sitting behind a very large, rather battered desk, his back toward her, leaning on the long credenza against the wall and holding a telephone in one hand, scribbling furiously with the other, obviously deeply involved in a business discussion.

He put his hand over the receiver and gave her a quick glance over his shoulder. "Be with you in a minute, Sarah," he said briefly, then turned back to continue his conversation.

While she waited for him to finish, Sarah inspected the room, which was as imposing as the outer offices, with fine furnishings, the same plush carpet, a large window on one wall, but also quite obviously a business office. Every available surface seemed to be covered with paper—files, account books, ledger sheets, correspondence, yellow legal pads—even the chairs.

She walked over to the window and stood gazing out at the panoramic view of the city, the Golden

Gate, the long, graceful bridge spanning it trying to calm her sudden attack of nerves. It hadn't worked out at all as she'd expected. After all, it was her first time in his office, and he hadn't even come to meet her himself. And who knew how long that conversation would go on? Still, they were finally going to be together, even if it was just a lunch, and would have a chance to talk at last.

"I'm sorry," she heard him say behind her just then.

"Oh, that's all right," she said, turning around and smiling at him. "I'm just so glad to see you..."

She broke off when she saw the expression on his face. He did a double take, his eyes widening then narrowing as he walked slowly toward her.

"Ross!" she exclaimed, alarmed. "Is something wrong?"

"Sarah?" he said, making it a question. "Is it really you?" He smiled then, but with an uncertain look in his eyes. "I hardly recognized you. What in the world have you done to yourself?"

She gave a nervous laugh and put a hand to her hair, stiff under its heavy layer of spray. "Oh, Sylvia's been helping me with my shopping, and I thought—that is, *we* thought—I might as well improve some other things to go with the new clothes. Don't you like it?"

"Well, yes," he said, still staring dubiously at her, his eyes flicking her up and down. "You look great, wonderful, in fact. You just took me by surprise, that's all." He laughed. "I *was* expecting the old Sarah. You can hardly blame me for gawking when I turn around to find this—this vision before my eyes, this glamorous sophisticate."

She gave him a troubled look. "You don't like it, I can tell."

He laughed again, put an arm around her shoulder and pulled her to him. "Of course I like it. It'll just take some getting used to." He dropped his arm and looked at his watch. "Now, shall we go get that lunch? I don't have much time. My plane leaves at three o'clock, and I still have some files to review."

The lunch was not a success. She'd been so looking forward to it and tried her best to get back on their former intimate footing, but he seemed so distracted, kept glancing at his watch, drumming his fingers on the table at any delay in the service, even speaking sharply to a clumsy waiter who spilled a few drops of water when he was pouring it.

Finally, when they'd finished eating and he'd called for the check, she reached across the table and put a hand on his arm, just as he'd started to rise from his chair.

"Ross, I've got an idea. Why don't I come to the airport to see you off? That'd give us a little more time together."

He frowned. "Oh, Sarah, that wouldn't work today. I'll have two of my assistants with me, and we'll be discussing business."

"Oh," she said in a small voice, her face falling.

"You do understand, don't you?"

"Yes, of course," she replied, forcing out a smile. "It's just that we hardly see each other anymore. I don't even know what your plans are."

"Plans?" he asked. "What plans?"

"Well, have you decided what you want to do? The last time we discussed it, you still seemed to feel you might be able to walk away from the business. Have you changed your mind?"

He heaved a sigh. "Sarah, now isn't the time to talk about that. I've been so wrapped up in this Los Angeles affair that I haven't had a minute to even think about anything else. Once it's over, just a few more weeks now, then I'll be able to give more serious thought to my future—our future. In the meantime, I'm going to have to ask you to be patient. In any event, I'll be here for the Van Ness bash on Saturday. We can talk then. All right?"

"Yes," she said in a tight voice. "I guess I'll just have to be patient." She got up. "Now, I can see you're anxious to leave."

For the rest of that day, something about his explanation nagged at the back of her mind, but it wasn't until several hours later, as she sat in the den with Sylvia half-watching a mindless quiz show, still troubled by the unsatisfactory lunch and Ross's initial reaction to her appearance, that it suddenly hit her.

He'd told her to be patient, assured her it would only be a few more weeks. She could do that, knew she must if she wanted to keep him. What had disturbed her, vaguely at the time but now leaping into her conscious mind, was something he'd said to her at the beach about his business affairs. She could almost quote him verbatim, hear his voice in her head. "It seems the minute I put out one fire, another has already sprung up behind me."

Would it always be like that? When he got his business in Los Angeles settled, would there be another issue that demanded all his attention, another fire to put out somewhere else? And could she live with that way of life if he did decide he had to stay?

On Saturday night, Sarah had just emerged from the shower when she heard a knock on her bedroom door. Throwing on a toweling robe, she ran to answer it. Sylvia was standing there, also in her robe, a scowl of irritation on her face.

"Oh, Sarah," she said, "Ross just called. He won't be able to pick you up for the party as planned. Apparently, he has to get there early. It seems Mr. Van Ness is involved in this business deal of his, and some bigwigs are up from L.A. to discuss it, too. Of course, Father is already there, as well. So I'm sorry, but it looks as though you'll have to go with me."

Sarah's heart plummeted, and she struggled to cover her dismay. "Don't worry about it, Sylvia," she replied. "It can't be helped. He *will* be there, I hope."

"Oh, yes. And I think you're great to be so understanding. I'm afraid if I were in your shoes . . ." Her voice trailed off and the frown deepened. "I love my brother," she went on, "but there are times I could cheerfully murder him."

Sarah had to laugh. "Oh, don't do that, Sylvia. Surely the meeting won't last all night."

Sylvia rolled her eyes. "One never knows." Then she grinned. "If anything can drag him away, it'll be that knockout new dress."

"I hope you're right. I'm still a little nervous about wearing it in public, though. It seems awfully revealing."

Sylvia cocked an eyebrow at her. "Be grateful you've got something to reveal," she commented dryly, pointing at her own flat chest and bony frame. "Besides, compared to what some of the others will be wearing, you'll feel positively Victorian."

The Van Ness mansion, perched at the very top of one of the city's steepest hills, in one of its most exclusive areas, was blazing with lights when they arrived a few hours later.

A uniformed valet opened the car doors for them, and they stepped out onto the wide pavement. Sylvia gripped Sarah by the arm and leaned over to murmur in her ear, "Now, there's not a thing in the world to be nervous about. You'll knock 'em all dead."

Sarah gave her a grateful smile, and they began to ascend the wide stone staircase that led to the imposing entrance. From inside came the sounds of an orchestra and a constant hum of raised voices, punctuated by loud bursts of laughter. More cars were already arriving behind them.

Actually, Sarah was so anxious to see Ross that she didn't have time to be nervous. She knew she looked her best, and these people didn't frighten her, not when her whole future was at stake. Her mind was firmly made up that she and Ross would have that talk, and it had to be tonight, business or no business.

Ever since their lunch date a few days ago, her concern over the course their relationship was taking had grown, until it verged by now on real desperation. Something had to be done. Her life here was empty, aimless. She was only drifting in a kind of vacuum, waiting for Ross to show up, to call, with nothing else to fill her thoughts during the long, boring days.

She missed her home at the beach dreadfully, her dull but contented existence there, the friends who really cared about her, her work, the marine life she'd devoted herself to for so long. It was also crystal clear to her now that Ross's immersion in his business affairs wouldn't end with this one transaction. After it was settled, another would arise to take its place, and she'd begun to doubt if she could tolerate spending the rest of her life on the fringes of his.

It was a far more serious problem than she had anticipated, but not an insoluble one, she was convinced. They loved each other, were committed to a future together. But if they didn't talk about it—and soon, tonight—she was afraid it might be too late.

They were greeted at the top of the stairs by a stout matron dressed in a black gown and resplendent with jewels, who was introduced to her as Mrs. Van Ness, their hostess. Then they made their way to an immense ballroom, where the orchestra was playing and people were dancing. A uniformed maid led them to their table, one of the choicest in the room.

They had left their coats with an attendant in the cloakroom on the way, and as Sarah glanced around the room, she could see that Sylvia hadn't been exaggerating when she'd claimed the other women's gowns would be even barer than her own. Still, she wasn't quite comfortable with her new image. She'd done it for Ross's sake, and now he wasn't even here.

As the two of them sat there sipping their wine, Sylvia pointed out various people to her, some of them quite famous. A senator, a retired cinema actress, a renowned artist, a prominent architect and, of course, several captains of industry whose names were not so well-known, but who actually wielded enormous power.

They were joined shortly by Michael, the doctor brother, and his wife, and the other sister, whose husband was also at the meeting in the library. Sarah listened to them chattering about their mutual acquaintances, the other women's gowns, arcane gossip. Her mind wandered, and she smiled inanely, feeling totally out of place.

Finally, she heard Michael raise his voice above the chatter of the women. "Well, here they come at last," he said with patent relief. "Looks like the meeting must be over."

Sarah glanced up quickly to see six men, dressed in black tuxedos, just coming into the ballroom from a side entrance, Ross at the head, his eyes searching the room. He looked wonderful, devastatingly handsome in his formal clothes, and Sarah half rose out of her chair, a hand raised to capture his attention.

Just then, a tall brunette, dressed in a flaming scarlet, form-fitting gown, stepped in front of him, blocking him from view. Staring in dismay, Sarah sank back on her chair as the woman put her arm through his and they moved together onto the dance floor.

"Oh, drat that blasted Laura Van Ness!" Sylvia hissed in her ear. "Leave it to her to pull one of her stunts, tonight of all nights." She leaned closer. "Listen, Sarah, it doesn't mean a thing. Even though they were never officially engaged, Laura still can't seem to give up. But it is her house, her father is an important player in this deal Ross is trying to put together, and he can't be rude to her."

"Yes," Sarah said, forcing out a tight smile, "I can see that." She pushed her chair back and rose to her feet, the false grin still in place. "Now, if you'll excuse me, I think I'll visit the powder room."

On her way, she couldn't resist one quick glance at the dance floor. She spotted them right away. Both Laura's arms were twined around Ross's neck, and they were barely swaying to the music, their bodies close together. Nor did Ross look as though he was suffering. He was smiling down at the lovely brunette, his arms clasped loosely around her waist, his face animated.

In fact, they looked exactly like they belonged together.

CHAPTER NINE

EXCEPT for the lone attendant, who was busy at one end of the long room folding towels, the powder room was blessedly empty. Sarah made her way quickly into a cubicle and locked the door behind her. She pulled down the lid of the commode and sat down on top of it, her eyes squeezed shut, trying to take deep, slow breaths to calm the wild beating of her heart.

A sickening wave of dizziness passed over her, so intense she was afraid she was about to faint. She bent down and put her head between her legs, and in a moment the nausea passed, her head cleared. She leaned back and closed her eyes again, her hands clutched tightly in her lap.

Her head still whirling, Sarah struggled to break free of the emotions that raged within her, to *think*. Even now, in the midst of her inner turmoil, she knew, with absolute clarity that it wasn't really Laura Van Ness that had caused it.

Although it had been terrible to see another woman in Ross's arms, acting as though she owned him, Sarah knew her reaction wasn't mere jealousy. It was only the catalyst that pushed her over the edge. The real problem went much deeper than that, to the very root of their relationship, and she was helpless against it. How could she combat an enemy she couldn't even see?

Just then, she heard someone come in, water running, women's voices speaking in hushed, intimate tones, and she rose quickly to her feet. It was time to leave, and even more imperative now that she and Ross have that talk tonight. She couldn't go on like this.

But just as she was about to unlatch the door, she heard one of the women mention his name, and she stood there, paralyzed, straining her ears to hear what they were saying.

"Did you get a look at Ross Kirk and Laura Van Ness on the dance floor just now?" one of them commented slyly.

"Oh, yes. Just like old times, wasn't it? I knew he wouldn't be able to keep Laura down for long. She always gets what she wants in the end. But what about the houseguest? Sarah something. Won't she present an obstacle?"

There came the sound of tinkling, scornful laughter. "You mean our little beach girl? Oh, she's just a passing whim of Ross's. You know how he is. Always has to be different. She's most likely the result of a mid-life crisis."

"Really? I thought it was pretty serious. She *did* save his life, from what I hear. And she *is* staying in Sylvia's house, you know, so the family must approve."

"Well, what else can they do? You mark my words. He may be grateful to her for saving his life, as you say, and the family may be indulging his whim by taking her in, but I mean, really, Angela. Have you seen those clothes? That hair? Can you picture her as Ross Kirk's wife, the hostess presiding over his dinner table?"

"Well, no, I guess not. But to be fair, she looks quite presentable tonight. Of course, I just saw her at a distance."

"Only skin-deep, my dear. You wait and see. It won't be long before Ross wakes up and sees her for what she is, a real liability."

More giggles. "And with Laura there in the wings moving things along, it can't miss." The voice lowered confidentially. "Besides which, I hear he's been down in L.A. most of the time since the beach girl arrived. Don't tell me a man like Ross Kirk is going to spend his evenings alone when he's out of town."

"Say, didn't he have a little fling not long ago with that actress? You know, the one who was in that film..."

Their voices trailed off, and Sarah heard the door to the outer room swish shut behind them. Her cheeks burning, her hands knotted into fists at her sides, she simply stood there for several long moments, replaying the hurtful conversation in her mind.

The worst thing about it was that, cruel as their words might be, they were right. Laura Van Ness and Ross *did* belong together. She'd thought so herself, seeing them on the dance floor. Apparently, everyone else did, too. How could she combat that kind of prejudice?

A fine anger began to simmer deep within her. Why bother even to try to fit into Ross's world if those two were any example of it? They'd referred to her as his "little beach girl." Well, so what? She had nothing to be ashamed of.

Suddenly, she knew what she had to do. The situation with Ross was hopeless. It wouldn't get any better. Her only recourse was to salvage what she could of her pride, her dignity, and return to her home, to friends who cared and accepted her as she was.

With a renewed sense of purpose, she asked the attendant for a pad and pencil, scribbled a quick note on it for Sylvia, saying she was unwell and would find her own way home. She asked the maid to call her a cab and gave her the note to deliver to Sylvia after she'd gone, tipping her handsomely.

Then she retrieved her coat and went outside to wait for the cab.

Back at Sylvia's, the big house deserted and deathly silent, Sarah sprinted up the stairs to her bedroom. She had to hurry. When Sylvia read her note, she just might come after her, or at least call to see how she was. In fact, just as she was struggling out of the gown, the telephone did ring. She ignored it and kept on.

She went to the closet and pushed aside all the new clothes she'd bought, reaching far in the back to where she'd relegated the ones she'd brought from home. She dressed hurriedly in her old navy blue suit. The awful sprayed hairstyle would have to wait. There was no time to wash it or scrub the makeup off her face.

When she'd finished packing her old familiar clothes into the battered suitcase, she carried it downstairs to the telephone and called a cab. The minute she hung up, it began ringing again. For a moment, she hesitated. It could be Ross. But what was there left to say? She'd written him a note, a short, succinct one, to be sure, but in it she'd said everything, and she went over it in her mind, the telephone still jangling in her ear.

"Dear Ross," she'd said. "Please don't think too badly of me for running like this. It was the only way I could do it. It's clear to me now that things could never work between us. I don't fit into your world and never will. Please don't try to contact me. It's better to make a clean break now."

She'd hesitated before signing it, then simply written "Sarah" at the bottom. There was nothing more to add.

When the cab finally arrived, she jumped into the back seat, filled with an enormous sense of relief. There was no way they could stop her now. "San Francisco Airport, please," she said, and the cab sped away into the dark night.

"You mean to say you just up and left?" Carol exclaimed, her eyes wide with shock.

It was just three days later, and the two women were sitting in Sarah's kitchen over a morning cup of coffee. It hadn't taken Carol long to nose out the fact that Sarah had come back—alone—and that her flight had been precipitate.

"Well, what else could I do?" Sarah asked. "Even if Ross had made the time to discuss the situation, it wouldn't have changed anything. So long as he stays there, tied to the family business, I'd stay on the fringes of his life. Try to understand, Carol. I was so bored I was afraid I'd lose my mind."

"I see. And you don't think seeing him dancing with this old flame of his had anything to do with your sudden decision?"

Sarah had pondered this question in her heart and mind almost constantly since she'd left. In all honesty, she had to admit it did have a devastating effect on her to see Laura Van Ness in Ross's arms, but that episode in itself would never have made her leave the way she did.

"I don't think so," she said slowly. "At least I hope not. Not only did I truly believe Ross wasn't interested in her, but even if she had presented a serious problem, another woman would have given me something real to fight." She shook her head. "No, Carol. I think I can honestly say that the real problem went much deeper than the sight of him dancing with an old girlfriend."

Carol was silent for a long time, sipping her coffee, frowning down at the table. Then she heaved a sigh and rose to her feet. She crossed over to Sarah and put a hand on her shoulder, giving it a friendly squeeze.

"I think you're probably right. You've never struck me as the jealous type. Besides, I'm delighted to have you back. I really missed you, kiddo. But right now, I've got to get going. Got a lunch meeting of the hospital volunteers at my house to get ready for."

Tears stung behind Sarah's eyes at her friend's kind words. Blinking them back, she put her hand over Carol's for a moment, then got up to walk with her to the door.

"What will you do now?" Carol asked as she stepped out onto the porch.

Sarah shrugged. "Finish up last year's report first of all. All the figures are in, and I have a pretty complete draft. Then, who knows? Later on, I might even consider going back to school, finishing up my degree, and try to go on with my father's work on my own. I stand a pretty good chance once I have some credentials."

"What a great idea!" Carol said admiringly. "I don't see why not. When did you decide that?"

"Well, I haven't really decided for sure yet," Sarah replied. "And actually it was Ross who gave me the idea."

"I see. So, he wasn't all bad."

"Oh, Carol, he wasn't bad at all. He's a wonderful man, more than I'd ever hoped for. If there was any way..." She stopped, choking on the words. "But there isn't," she added dully.

"And what about Timothy? Do you see him in your future at all?"

Sarah shook her head vigorously. "Oh, no. And to pretend I did would be unfair to both of us."

"Well, you've set yourself a tough course in life, kiddo, but if anyone can do it, I think you can. Now, I'm off to fix lunch for my ladies. I'll call you later."

Sarah stood at the door for a long time watching her friend scurry down the path, then make the turn that led up the beach to her own house, until she finally disappeared from view. Then she turned and went slowly back to the kitchen to pour herself another cup of coffee, the tears falling unchecked now that she was alone.

She'd never dreamed she'd miss Ross so much, the sound of his voice, his sheer physical presence.

The ache in her heart wouldn't go away no matter how she tried to justify leaving him. His love had changed her in a way that was permanent. She could never go back now to the way she was before he came along. And he *had* loved her. Of that she was certain. And that was precisely what made the whole thing so painful.

She stood at the window gazing out at the bleak gray day. It was raining, a cold, sleety drizzle that could turn to snow, not unusual even at the beach in late December. She could hardly believe the old year was almost over. And what a year it had been! Her father dying, then Ross coming into her life. Inwardly, she had changed so drastically that it seemed it should show on the surface, as well. Yet when she looked in the mirror, it was the same old Sarah Wainwright she saw reflected back at her.

The first thing she'd done when she arrived home early on the morning after her flight was to get under the shower, wash her hair clean of the spray and scrub all the makeup off her face. She hadn't been able to catch a flight to Seattle until five o'clock in the morning and had sat in the San Francisco airport terrified, yet still half-hoping, that Ross would come after her.

But he hadn't. Which meant he must have seen the wisdom of her decision, must have realized it would never work. She'd been all wrong for him from the beginning, had even kept making mistakes, especially trying to improve her image. She'd never forget the look on his face the day she'd gone to his office to have lunch with him.

She'd made a heroic effort to appear suitable for the part he wanted her to play in his life, the wife

of a busy executive, socially acceptable in his
exalted circles, yet there was no mistaking the look
of distaste on his face when he'd first seen her in
her new image. He'd covered it up quickly, but it
had been there.

Yet, she told herself, as she rinsed out the cups
and coffeemaker at the kitchen sink, wasn't that
just further proof that it never would never worked?
Ross had fallen in love with the Sarah he had met
at the beach. Take her out of that environment and
she was like one of her beloved porpoises who had
to live in the sea or die.

Christmas came and went. Sarah attended Carol's
annual open house as usual, and even though her
heart still felt fragile, she managed to get through
the evening smiling and chatting with her old
friends. But when Timothy kissed her under the
mistletoe, a friendly, almost brotherly brush of his
lips on hers, the ache only intensified, and she made
her excuses early.

After a few weeks of cold clear weather in early
January, Sarah awoke one morning to a bleak and
forbidding gray sky. A heavy bank of black clouds
was moving in fast from the south, and by
afternoon a brisk breeze had come up.

By four o'clock, it had turned into a full-blown
gale, with the wind howling in the trees outside, the
surf pounding wildly against the shore. It looked
as though a major storm could be brewing, just
like the one last autumn. She stood at the kitchen
window gazing out at the tall firs and hemlock
swaying in the terrific wind, wondering if she should

go out in it and batten down the hatches while it was still light. Of course, it could pass over by nightfall as they sometimes did.

She decided to wait. After a light early supper, she took a long, hot bath, then built a fire in the living room. She sat in front of it, drinking a cup of coffee and reading through the final version of the yearly migration report she had finally finished. It was already overdue, and she wanted to get it mailed the next day.

But she couldn't concentrate. The storm still raging outside kept distracting her, and she wished now she'd prepared for it that afternoon. She really should get out the camp stove, the kerosene lamps and candles while the electricity was still working.

Just then, she heard a loud clatter at the side of the house. It sounded as though one of the chairs she'd left out on the patio was blowing up against the house. So, when she heard the garden gate banging, she knew she'd have to go outside and secure them both before the chair broke a window or the gate blew off its hinges.

With a sigh, she got up and went into the kitchen to get the heavy-duty torch, then shrugged into her heavy jacket, tied a scarf around her head and ran outside.

She retrieved the chair first, then ran down the path to fasten the gate. But just as she was heading back to the house, her head bent against the force of the wind, she heard the sound of an automobile engine out on the road, barely audible above the howling in the trees.

Wondering who on earth would be foolish enough to venture out on the road in such weather, she turned around to see headlights coming closer, the heavy rain visible in their glare. Then, to her amazement, the car swept into her own driveway. When she shone the torch in that direction, she saw a man get out, then come walking toward her.

She stood there, gaping, as he came into the torch's glare and she recognized him. It was Ross, his hair ruffled in the wind, his hands in the pockets of his anorak, his eyes fastened firmly on her.

"Well, Sarah," he said when he reached her, "aren't you going to offer me shelter from the storm?"

Sarah's heart was thudding so hard by now that she didn't think she could even speak, much less move. Finally, Ross gripped her firmly by the arm and started leading her toward the house. All she could do was follow along wordlessly.

By the time they were inside, the door closed against the wind and rain, she'd recovered from the shock somewhat, but still couldn't seem to find her voice. She turned to him just inside the hallway and looked searchingly up into his face. His expression was totally blank, as though he was waiting for her to make the next move.

"What are you doing here?" she finally managed to croak.

"I came to see you."

"But why?"

He shrugged, the ghost of a smile playing around his lips. "Why not? We're old friends, aren't we? Let's just say I was in the neighborhood, and when the storm came up, I decided to stop by." Then his face hardened, and when he spoke again, there was a grim edge to his voice. "Why in God's name did you leave me like that, Sarah?"

She turned away from him, unable to face those penetrating gray eyes. Her mind and heart were in turmoil, torn between the joy of seeing him and the pain of having to go through the torment of losing him a second time.

"I thought it was best," she finally replied in a low voice.

"*You* thought!" he shouted angrily. "And what about me? Didn't my thoughts, my feelings, matter a damn to you?"

Startled by the sudden fury in his voice, she turned back to him. His face was livid, his mouth set in a grim line, a little pulse beating along his unshaven jaw. It dawned on her then for the first time that he was hurting, too! Somehow that had never occurred to her. He'd always seemed such a tower of strength, so self-assured, almost invulnerable.

"Ross," she stammered, "I'm sorry if I hurt you. I didn't mean to. I honestly thought it was better for you if I left. I told you that in my note. I can't fit into your world, and you obviously can't leave it behind. What else could I do?"

"You could have talked to me about it!" he ground out.

"I tried!" she cried, growing angry herself by now. "How many times did I tell you we needed to talk, and how many times did you put me off?"

Scowling, he dropped his gaze, and a surge of satisfaction ran through her. She'd struck a nerve that time! But her pleasure was short-lived. The

haunting look of real pain on his face went straight
to her heart.

"Can't you see?" she said in a gentler tone. "It
never would have worked. We come from almost
different species." It was on the tip of her tongue
to tell him about the conversation she'd overheard
in the Van Ness powder room, which had only confirmed her own fears about her total unsuitability
as Ross's wife, but stopped herself just in time.
What good would it do?

Why had he come? What did he want of her?
When the storm blew over he'd leave, and that
would be the end of it. In the meantime, she'd just
have to bear with his presence. The one thing she
must not do was allow herself to be seduced back
into loving him, wanting him, hoping.

"Come on," she said with a sigh. "Come into
the kitchen. You can't go back out in that storm.
I can at least make you a cup of coffee." She started
toward the kitchen, glancing over her shoulder at
him. "Have you had supper?"

He hadn't moved, was still standing there, his
eyes fixed on the floor. Finally, he raised his head.
His face looked smoothed over, and the anger
seemed to have drained out of him at last.

"No, I haven't," he replied dully.

"Well, I'd better feed you something before you
leave." She tried to make her voice light and cheery.
"With any luck, the storm will blow over soon. In
fact, it sounds as though the wind might be dying
down already."

He gave her one searching look, then nodded
shortly and followed her into the kitchen.

Still trying to keep up a running light patter, telling him about finishing her project, the latest whale sightings far to the north, village gossip, Carol's Christmas party, she kept her eyes firmly averted as she stood at the stove warming up the pot of soup for him. All the while, he didn't utter a word.

"And how was your Christmas?" she asked brightly as she poured out his soup and set the bowl down on the table before him.

"Rotten," he said shortly.

Then, before she could move away, he'd reached out to grip her firmly around the arm, his fingers biting into her flesh.

"Ross!" she cried, startled. "You're hurting me!"

"Good!" he exclaimed. "I should beat you." Then, relaxing his hold slightly, he looked up at her with such anguish in his eyes that she couldn't break away.

"Sarah, Sarah," he said in a low voice, shaking his head slowly from side to side. "I realize now how I must have hurt you. But didn't it ever occur to you how devastating the power you had over me could be? Couldn't you see that this great life of mine you were so worried about fitting into was only ashes without you in it?"

She could hardly believe her ears. For a man like Ross to humble himself this way was unthinkable. In spite of all her firm resolutions, she couldn't stop herself from reaching out to put a hand on his cheek, the stubble rasping under her fingers.

"Then why didn't you say so?" she asked softly. "Why wouldn't you even discuss it with me? Surely you must have seen how unhappy I was, how frustrated, never seeing you, always being put off for the sake of your business. I *had* no life there.''

"All right," he said. "I admit it was largely my fault. I should have made time to talk to you. But I honestly though you'd adjust in time. In fact, when you showed up at my office that day in your new finery, I was convinced you'd done so already." He gave her the ghost of a smile. "To tell you the truth, I was a little disappointed when I saw what you'd turned yourself into."

So she had been right! "Well, why didn't you say something then?"

"Because that damned business deal had me so frantic I couldn't think of anything else. I'd fallen back into the same old trap. I just didn't realize it."

"Yes," she said. "But I thought it was what you wanted."

"It was what I came up here last autumn to get free of!" he exclaimed. "I told you that at the time."

"But you didn't, did you? Get free?"

He shook his head. "No, I'm afraid not. I got sucked right back in. And I'd still be there if the price hadn't been too high."

She frowned. "The price? What price?"

"Losing you," he said quietly.

Their eyes met then, and Sarah felt as though she were melting, drowning in those gray depths. He was tugging gently but firmly at her arm now, and all at once he pulled her down onto his lap and his arms came around her.

"I love you, Sarah," he said, his eyes still locked on hers. "And you were right to go, in a way. It took losing you to make me realize just how much I loved you, needed you. I'd never needed anyone in my life that way before. I think it even frightened me a little. Actually, that's one reason I waited so long to come after you.'' He shook his head. ''I didn't like anyone having that kind of power over me.''

''And what were the other reasons?'' she asked, basking in the glow of his closeness, the feel of his strong arms holding her.

He smiled. ''I had some loose ends to finish up with the business before I left. For good this time.''

Her eyes widened, and she sat up straight, gazing at him, in shock. ''But what will you do? How will you live?''

He shrugged. ''I have some money of my own.''

''But you'd never be happy idle. You need work to do.''

''Oh, I haven't cut the ties completely.'' He gathered her to him more closely and tucked her hand under his chin, stroking her hair as he spoke. ''Here's what I think we should do. There's a great marine biology department at the university in San Francisco. I already checked it out. They know your father's work quite well and tell me that if you finish your degree, they'd be delighted to have you continue his work on your own, perhaps even teach.''

''That sounds wonderful,'' she said in a muffled voice, her heart full to bursting. ''But it still doesn't answer the question of your work, your future.''

''Just bear with me, and I'll explain. I've put my sister's husband into my old position. He's not really ready for it, but with my father's help he'll do just fine in time. I told them I'd work with him myself occasionally and help them out as a kind of troubleshooter, at least while you're in school. I figure we can spend part of the year in the city, the rest at the beach, at least during the spring and fall migrations, when it's important for you to be here."

Sarah sat up straight again and stared at him in utter astonishment. "And you've worked this out all by yourself?"

He nodded. "Subject to your approval, of course. Well? How does it sound to you?"

"It sounds perfect—for me. But I'm still concerned about your work. Will it be enough for you?"

"Well, when we're here at the beach, I can help you with your projects. In fact, I might even take a few of those classes with you. It's an interesting field." Then he reddened slightly and gave her a rather sheepish look. "To tell you the truth—and I've never mentioned this to another living soul—there *is* something I've always wanted to try."

"Well, what is it?" she asked, smiling.

He glowered at her. "Don't laugh now, or I *will* beat you. I want to paint."

"Paint? What do you mean? Houses? Fences?"

"You're laughing," he accused, giving her a stern look.

"I'm sorry. It just sounds so—so unlike you. Somehow I never thought of you as having an artistic streak."

"I'm not saying I want to be another Michelangelo. I'm actually more interested in architectural drawing, nature sketches, that kind of thing. Perhaps we could even put together a book one day. You provide the text, I do the illustrations. I was rather good at that kind of thing as a boy, and it's always interested me. Of course,'' he added casually, "we'll get married as soon as possible. Well? What do you think?''

She gazed deeply into his eyes. ''I think you're wonderful. I think I love you more than life itself. And I think I want you to kiss me. Now.''

His arm tightened around her, and she closed her eyes as his mouth came down on hers, gently at first, then hardening, drawing in her lips, then forcing them open. Her arms went around his neck and she pressed herself toward him, running her hands up into his dark, thick hair, her fingers raking through the crisp strands, every nerve in her body flaming now.

He tore his mouth away from hers then, to set her on her feet, and rose up to stand before her, putting his hands on her shoulders. She looked wordlessly up into his eyes, hooded and gleaming with desire. Slowly, his gaze never faltering, his hands slipped down her body, lingering over her straining breasts, bare underneath the thin material of her robe, then down to fumble with the tie at her waist.

''I want to see you, Sarah,'' he rasped thickly.

She drew in her breath sharply and nodded, giving him tacit permission to do whatever he wanted with her. She stood motionless, scarcely able to breathe, as he untied the robe, then reached up to slip it off her shoulders and down her arms until it fell loosely on the floor at her feet.

Her skin burned under his hungry gaze, and she lifted her chin slightly to mask the sudden shyness. His hands reached out to cover her breasts, the strong, tapering fingers molding the soft fullness. She moaned deep in her throat as his thumbs began circling around and around the taut peaks, her momentary embarrassment gone in the sheer pleasure of his warm touch.

Then, almost in a frenzy, she began to unbutton his shirt, until his chest was bare. Moving the material aside, she leaned down to touch the warm, bare skin with her lips. She could feel the sudden rapid beating of his heart, the strong muscles quivering under her mouth as it moved over his body.

Shrugging quickly out of his shirt, he gathered her to him, crushing her breasts against his strong, bare chest. "Let's go to bed, darling," he murmured in her ear.

Suddenly, the lights went out, and they made their way in total darkness down the hall to her bedroom, Ross guiding her from behind, pressed closely up against her, his arms firmly around her waist.

When they reached the side of the bed, one hand came up to move lightly, tantalizingly over her breasts, and the other slid downward over her stomach, her hips, her thighs. She leaned back against him in a mindless ecstasy, giving herself up completely to his exploring hands and the shafts of sensuous pleasure coursing through her.

Slowly, he turned her around to face him and looked down into her eyes. "I love you, Sarah," he said. "I want you more than I've ever wanted anything in my life. I was dead inside, and you've brought me back to life."

"I love you, too, Ross," she breathed. "So much more than I ever dreamed possible."

She hesitated for a second, then, daringly, her fingers began to fumble at the buckle of his belt. His hands dropped loosely to his sides, and he stood motionless, looking intently at her as she tugged at the dark trousers, pulling them down over his lean hips and long legs, then running her hands back up slowly along the muscled calves, covered with coarse hair, over the flat, hard stomach, until once again her arms twined around his neck and she arched her body closely up against him, joyously aware of his hard, aching need of her.

With a groan, his arms came around her, his lips claimed hers once more, his tongue thrusting, probing the soft interior of her mouth, and they sank slowly down onto the bed.

When they were joined together at last, Sarah gave herself to him totally, meeting his pulsing need with wild abandon, secure now in the knowledge that he loved her completely.

At first dawn the next morning, Sarah awoke to pale sunshine coming in through the bedroom window. Still half-asleep, she stretched contentedly, and as she did so, she felt a heaviness on her body, an arm thrown across her, a large hand clasping her possessively.

Memory came flooding back, and with a little smile, she glanced over at the dark head of the man lying beside her, his long body curled against her. She could feel his even breath on her skin, the steady heartbeat under her arm.

Carefully, so as not to disturb him and shatter the precious moment, she reached over and gently smoothed the dark hair, tousled over his forehead now in sleep. He stirred slightly, and the hand on her waist tightened as he shifted closer to her, his mouth nuzzling the hollow of her neck under her jaw.

Then he opened his eyes, blinked, and looked up at her, smiling. "Good morning, darling," he said in a low voice. He raised himself up on one elbow and bent down to kiss her lightly on the mouth. The hand began moving now, traveling over her breast. Then suddenly, he cocked his head, listening. "The wind has died down," he said. "The storm seems to have blown over."

"Yes," she said, smiling up at him. "So it has."

HARLEQUIN®

Don't miss these Harlequin favorites by some of our most
distinguished authors!
And now, you can receive a discount by ordering two or more titles!

HT#25645	THREE GROOMS AND A WIFE by JoAnn Ross	$3.25 U.S. ☐	
		$3.75 CAN. ☐	
HT#25647	NOT THIS GUY by Glenda Sanders	$3.25 U.S. ☐	
		$3.75 CAN. ☐	
HP#11725	THE WRONG KIND OF WIFE by Roberta Leigh	$3.25 U.S. ☐	
		$3.75 CAN. ☐	
HP#11755	TIGER EYES by Robyn Donald	$3.25 U.S. ☐	
		$3.75 CAN. ☐	
HR#03416	A WIFE IN WAITING by Jessica Steele	$3.25 U.S. ☐	
		$3.75 CAN. ☐	
HR#03419	KIT AND THE COWBOY by Rebecca Winters	$3.25 U.S. ☐	
		$3.75 CAN. ☐	
HS#70622	KIM & THE COWBOY by Margot Dalton	$3.50 U.S. ☐	
		$3.99 CAN. ☐	
HS#70642	MONDAY'S CHILD by Janice Kaiser	$3.75 U.S. ☐	
		$4.25 CAN. ☐	
HI#22342	BABY VS. THE BAR by M.J. Rodgers	$3.50 U.S. ☐	
		$3.99 CAN. ☐	
HI#22382	SEE ME IN YOUR DREAMS by Patricia Rosemoor	$3.75 U.S. ☐	
		$4.25 CAN. ☐	
HAR#16538	KISSED BY THE SEA by Rebecca Flanders	$3.50 U.S. ☐	
		$3.99 CAN. ☐	
HAR#16603	MOMMY ON BOARD by Muriel Jensen	$3.50 U.S. ☐	
		$3.99 CAN. ☐	
HH#28885	DESERT ROGUE by Erine Yorke	$4.50 U.S. ☐	
		$4.99 CAN. ☐	
HH#28911	THE NORMAN'S HEART by Margaret Moore	$4.50 U.S. ☐	
		$4.99 CAN. ☐	

(limited quantities available on certain titles)

	AMOUNT	$
DEDUCT:	**10% DISCOUNT FOR 2+ BOOKS**	$
ADD:	**POSTAGE & HANDLING**	$
	($1.00 for one book, 50¢ for each additional)	
	APPLICABLE TAXES*	$_____
	TOTAL PAYABLE	$_____
	(check or money order—please do not send cash)	

To order, complete this form and send it, along with a check or money order for the
total above, payable to Harlequin Books, to: **In the U.S.:** 3010 Walden Avenue,
P.O. Box 9047, Buffalo, NY 14269-9047; **In Canada:** P.O. Box 613, Fort Erie, Ontario,
L2A 5X3.

Name: _____

Address: _____ City: _____

State/Prov.: _____ Zip/Postal Code: _____

*New York residents remit applicable sales taxes.
 Canadian residents remit applicable GST and provincial taxes.
Look us up on-line at: http://www.romance.net

HBACK-JM4

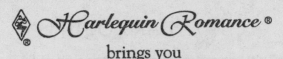

Harlequin Romance ®

brings you

SIMPLY THE BEST

Authors you'll treasure, books you'll want to keep!

Harlequin Romance books just keep getting better and better...and we're delighted to welcome you to our **Simply the Best** showcase for 1997, highlighting a special author each month!

Watch for:
#3451 ANGEL BRIDE
by Barbara McMahon

Angel had loved Jake but, without a word, he'd left. Now, two years later, Angel's life is at risk and Jake is back. But while Jake might protect her person, heaven knows what he'll do to her heart....

"Be prepared to be completely absorbed... Another winner from Ms. McMahon." *—Rendezvous*

"A fast-paced romantic suspense...a fun reading experience." *—Affaire de Coeur*

"An incredibly delightful and romantic tale. The reader will devour this book." *—Booklovers*

Available in April wherever Harlequin books are sold.

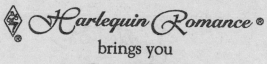

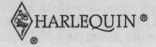